T0369947

DON'T THINK

JOHNS HOPKINS: POETRY AND FICTION
John T. Irwin, General Editor

Don't Think

Stories by Richard Burgin

JOHNS HOPKINS UNIVERSITY PRESS   Baltimore

This book has been brought to publication with the generous
assistance of the Poetry and Fiction Fund and the Writing
Seminars Publication Fund.

Johns Hopkins University Press
2715 North Charles Street
Baltimore, Maryland 21218-4363
www.press.jhu.edu

Library of Congress Cataloging-in-Publication Data

Burgin, Richard.
  [Short stories. Selections]
  Don't think : stories / by Richard Burgin.
    pages; cm.—(Johns Hopkins: poetry and fiction)
  ISBN 978-1-4214-1971-8 (pbk. : alk. paper)—ISBN 978-
1-4214-1972-5 (electronic)—ISBN 1-4214-1971-8 (pbk. : alk.
paper)—ISBN 1-4214-1972-6 (electronic)
  I. Title.
  PS3552.U717A6 2016
  813'.54   dc23   2015030267

A catalog record for this book is available from the British Library.

*Special discounts are available for bulk purchases of this book. For
more information, please contact Special Sales at 410-516-6936 or
specialsales@press.jhu.edu.*

FOR JOHN T. IRWIN

CONTENTS

DON'T THINK

Don't Think

Don't think of the roses on the trellis overhead—you motoring through, captain of your tricycle. Don't think of the birdbath either—where robins and blue jays drank or just rested—nor of the giant copper beech tree near it that you later climbed until you could enter your house through your bedroom window. It was also by the birdbath that you sometimes sang those first songs you learned in school like "At the Gates of Heaven" or, later, "Volare." Songs that seemed to have spread over the entire earth. Don't remember either the red rubber ball you'd throw against the garage wall or sometimes off its roof while you played imaginary baseball games with yourself or eventually with your friends. In right field was the enormous weeping willow tree that you used to climb with your sister and, to the right of that, the bright yellow forsythia bushes. Everything was large and bright in your backyard, even the gray cement patio from which you had snowball fights.

Your house had three floors (not counting its mysterious cellar) and twenty-one rooms, each one more like a district of a city than a mere room. Your sister's bedroom was opposite yours and next to the upstairs den. Adjacent to that was your father's

1

room, separated by the television room (from which you had a clear view of the schoolyard) from your mother's room. Why did they have separate rooms? Don't think of how much older he was than your mother and how you also were a father late in life. Don't think of how you ran in frenzied circles from your sister's room one night. You had been shocked by what you saw there when you'd barged in unannounced to sharpen your pencil. Your sister and another girl were lying naked in bed. You finally ran into your mother's room. Forget that your mother guessed what it was without your telling her—her special kind of knowledge. Don't remember either the many times you lay on your mother's bed holding her white French poodle while she practiced her violin, or how, when she was finished, she'd lay next to you. Don't think of all your mother's kisses or of the time you couldn't sleep because you were either too hot or too cold and your father stayed by your bed lifting up the blanket and then lowering it until you finally fell asleep. Don't realize you will never be loved that way again.

The sun-room, the music room with its grand piano, and outside a hill you could sled down in the winter snow with your sister and at the bottom look up at the two rows of cement stairs with their black railing above them like the mane of a frozen horse. Those stairs that led to the front of the house, a house that looked like a palace.

But one day you'd look at the music room windows to the right of the front door and you'd remember your mother making you repeat the same little piece until every note was perfect. Meanwhile, your friends were at the schoolyard waiting for you to play with them. Yet she made you repeat every note until it was 100% correct. You can still see how you cried then—a waterfall of tears—until it ended with her, at last, relenting. Later, your father told her not to force you to play the piano and she agreed and so you had the last real lesson of your life from your mother that day when you were seven years old and didn't become a great musician like them. The whole course of your life was determined in an afternoon. Your parents were both child prodigies, but you would never study music, though you tried briefly a few other times. And although you later made up scores of songs and little piano pieces, you never learned to read or write music and eventually could only play seven or eight of your pieces by memory as time went on because what isn't written down gets forgotten. Don't think of that world of music, lost in that music room in a house that's now lost as well.

It was shortly after you realized you would never become a real composer that you began thinking about infinity and the limits of consciousness. It began, perhaps, from a passage in Eliot's *Four Quartets*: "human kind / cannot bear very much reality." It was surprising that such a passage ever escaped from an Anglican monarchist who no doubt believed in heaven. But don't think of Eliot. He was only a fearful man, a fleeting speck, afraid like everyone else, taking shelter under his house of faith, blotting out reality himself, of course. Don't think of Borges or Beckett, either. Don't think of literature, the most pathetic of all religions, with its church of art that enforces the belief that great art will endure forever. Don't think of how we constantly misuse words like "forever" without grasping their meaning. We could not bear it if we did. And avoid the thought that if the world ends we'll lose everything in art including Shakespeare and Beethoven but if the world goes on forever they'll be lost and forgotten as well. "Art is the last illusion," your father once said to you, and all these years later you see that he was right. Don't think of him—the only man you ever trusted. Don't think

3

of what his life was like with all its struggles and heartbreak and what it did or didn't mean. It was he who led you to the paradox of paradoxes: "How can there always have been something; how could there ever have been nothing?" But don't think of that, and don't ever speak of it again to your son who told you he didn't like it, that it gave him a headache. Don't think of how much you miss him while he's at his mother's and how much more you'll miss him when he'll inevitably move out in a year or two.

Above all, don't go through your Rolodex again. Stop it! It's just an escape. For you to have handwritten cards in this age of the Internet is ridiculous. It's especially painful to see the names and numbers you wrote by hand as if your handwriting somehow makes the dead ones seem alive. Don't think of how some of them are looking at your name and wondering if you are dead. If you had been famous then they would have at least known that. Better to let the TV swallow more of your time, which is its main purpose on this earth. Don't think of the earth—how little of it you've seen or will ever see. Don't hear Mahler's "Das Lied von der Erde" in your head again. How did Mahler live for fifty years without losing his mind? Don't think of Mahler.

Don't think of the great painters either. Stop wondering how many of the old ones' fingers began to tremble as yours do now and how it affected their painting. It's a good thing you weren't a painter. But it would also be the same for pianists, if you had become one. Don't think of your own occasionally trembling fingers or of the times they used to bring you pleasure. Don't think of all the time you spent on women—pursuing them, placating them, cajoling them, every word in the world you can think of with them, trying to forgive the things they said, or didn't, that hurt you, or all the guilt you felt for the things you did to them. Don't think of your marriage or of your divorce, or of your first girlfriend who stayed overnight with you in your house when your parents and sister were away and with whom you lost your virginity in your mother's bed. Don't think of how it foretold in microcosm all the women that were in your future. It was like a single tree foretelling a forest one hundred yards ahead. Don't think of how the women all eventually scattered like the seeds of trees. A single wink and they've gone with the wind. Don't remember how you mourned the ones you loved nor all the time you spent looking at the photographs you took of them and the places where you took them, often by the ocean. You were so much stronger then. You could teach, play basketball, and make love in the same day! Don't think of how strong you once were and how your body slowly and then more rapidly declined. First you needed glasses, no, first your hair began to thin, no, first you started losing teeth, then your hair began to get a little gray, then it thinned, then your gums began to bleed, then your legs began to ache on airplanes or sitting in the movies. Is that right? You can never be sure when it comes to reconstructing your deconstruction. Everything in a sense was destruction, only your son is creation (although destined to ultimately be destroyed, both he and his work, like all other living things, no matter how great they both may be). Like your father, you had him late in life, so surely you can at least receive the gift of dying before he does. Don't worry about the fate of his work.

It's deeply ironic how people believe art expands consciousness and therefore life when it actually does the opposite. Anything with a design, with a beginning, middle, and end, is in opposition to infinity (or reality) and therefore is purposely a lie and a colossal deception. Art is the last illusion. Don't wonder why your father told you this, you'll never know.

Don't think of the days you've lost with your son, days that you loved so much which can never be repeated. You wrote stories and songs about him but none of them capture a scintilla of him. Photographs a little, perhaps videos some more, but really they capture very little. You think of the walks you took in the country. The spontaneous decisions you both made about whether to go to the barn or go to where the pine needles were. You could not have your mind on a camera then, how could you, any more than you could have when you two were leaping over waves in Santa Barbara or Atlantic City. It is doubtful you will ever do this again, although there is hope perhaps from the aquatic therapy you're doing. Maybe you two can one day go to a swimming pool in town about a mile from you, but you'll probably never again swim in the unfettered waves you both loved. Don't think of all the things you'll never do with him again. No more hide-and-seek, no more holding his hand as you cross the street, never again will he come into your room and lie next to you in bed because he was scared to be alone, never again will you take a bath together. During one bath he pointed to his penis and asked you "Does it fall off?" You wanted to say, "Not if you meet the right woman," but of course you answered his question as earnestly as it was asked.

With each year past the age of ten he began to withdraw more and more from other kids and from the very outdoors. First fewer and fewer bike rides, then no more walks to the playground, no more playing on the playground, then fewer and fewer sled rides or playing in the snow, as if the snow had somehow become contaminated. "The outdoors is so twentieth century," he'd say as he began to spend more and more time in his room at his computer looking up facts about countries—their populations, their governments, their predominant religions, their economies, weather, history, topography, lakes, and rivers, as if he were secretly commanded to memorize the world. And whenever he needed a break from his self-directed research he would start bouncing a ball over and over. Meanwhile, he had only one friend, the daughter of his mother's best friend who lived miles away and who he saw less and less as he got older until she started to seem as imaginary as the characters you and he told stories about every day you were together. Stories complete with a multitude of characters. First animals, then humans living in imaginary countries like Rhodnesia and Rudolpha, Blubberland and Rationalia, all parts of the continent Crasia. All of this he drew on incredibly detailed maps. When he was younger he drew some wonderful pictures of people, but now all his skill goes into the maps of imaginary countries or cities. He also used to write poetry, but now all his verbal skills and imagination go into the story you two tell each other when you're together.

Of course you wish you could do other things. You especially wish you could still travel with him. You two went to Paris, London, the Netherlands, Poland, Canada, Spain, the Czech Republic, and many places in the United States as well. Only then would he forgo his computer and sightsee, or go swimming, or once in California climb part of a mountain with you.

Your legs are not strong enough, not pain-free enough, to travel now, but he never says a word about it. Unlike you, he has an aversion to discussing (and probably even thinking about) painful things. Don't think about how much less demanding and how much more patient and uncomplaining he is than you. With the way you treated women your whole life, you don't deserve a person as good as him. The truth is all you really need to be happy is to talk with him, to watch him run up and down the hall as you two tell the story, arms waving by his sides.

Don't worry about how secretive he is; you were secretive,

too. When he was very young he said "I'm different," and you told him you were different as well. Another time he told you "Sometimes I don't mind hiding from you." He was so open then! But you also at times hid from him. You used to sometimes hide behind a tree and watch him on the schoolyard during recess. All the other kids were talking or playing with each other, but he would always be running by himself in a straight line back and forth over and over until recess ended.

Don't think of how little he brags or tries to call attention to himself, unlike you, who spent so much of your life trying to get attention, trying to impress your father and mother and then everyone else you met and then through your work people you hadn't met or wouldn't ever meet. You, despite believing in infinity, in the eventual, absolute disappearance of all people and all things, sought attention for your work anyway. Not to mention your lifelong attempt to get attention from women. Don't think of how honest your son is, unlike you, who used to sneak into your father's room and steal change from his pants or the pockets of the coats hanging in his closet. You stole from him although your father was the most generous person with money you ever knew. Don't think of how much you've worried about your son his whole life and still continue to. Would he grow enough, would he be ridiculed or bullied by other kids? Would his mother be careful enough with him when they went swimming, would he ever have a friend, get a job, be loved by anyone outside his family? He laughs at how much you worry and yet you continue to. You've never told him how anxious you get that you somehow won't see him on the days he's supposed to be with you. That his mother won't bring him on time (although she always has brought him, if sometimes a little late). The nervous feeling that this will happen begins about an hour before she's supposed to drop him off. You are feeling it now because he's supposed to be here in fifty-five minutes. You try to reassure yourself, but you feel it anyway. You know you must never tell anyone about this. You figure it's merely one of the forms of your craziness. Still, your son seems to know this about you.

"Don't be such an obsessive Wad," he'll say to you. You and he call each other "Gofus" and "Wad," though you claim to be from Rudolpha, a country whose motto is "Safety first, children first, beauty always," a country that won't let children into R-rated movies until they are thirty-five. At times when your son tells you you're acting "especially Wadish," he contends that you have "dual citizenship" with Wadovia.

Don't think of how you two never fight, how you haven't even raised your voice to him once in over three years. It's different with his mother, with whom he sometimes quarrels. In that way he's repeating what happened to you as a child. You would fight with your mother but were also much more affectionate with her than with your father, with whom you rarely fought. On the other hand, a lot of your son's affection with his mother is instigated by her. You've seen her force him to hug her at times. Which is good because he needs to be mainstreamed a bit. Don't think of how innocent he still is. It will break your heart.

Don't think of how you had to stop kissing him goodnight a few years ago or how you always have to initiate the good-bye hugs before his mother takes him on a long trip. Don't think of how much happier the three of you could have been if you all could have lived together. You tried, perhaps not as hard as you could have, but you tried.

There's a name for what his condition is—there are always names, although names are being replaced more and more by initials until the world becomes a giant labyrinth of confusion as the number of initials continues to grow exponentially while we forget more and more what they stand for. Anyway, he must have heard you talking to a doctor or a teacher on the phone because later he said, "What's Asparagus Syndrome?" You could honestly say, "It's a vegetable, so I guess you could say it's part of the vegetable syndrome." There are names for everything, though they will also all disappear because of the forces of infinity just like everything else.

But infinity or not, you have to get through the next forty-seven minutes until your son gets dropped off—assuming his mother brings him on time. Don't think of all the things that could happen to keep him from coming to you. Sometimes you get into a kind of magical thinking and believe if you do a good or generous thing it will increase your odds of seeing him on time. You once sent a girlfriend named Justine, whom you mistreated, a thousand-dollar check and have been meaning to send her another one. There would still be time for you to put it in the mailbox a block or two away if you act promptly. After all, there is no one you ever treated worse than her—as bad, once or twice, but never worse—and those other women you've lost touch with; one of them no longer even lives in America. The problem with Justine is you can't be sure of her address and would have to call her first, which you dread.

Do something productive for once during these forty-six minutes while you still have to wait. Look through your Rolodex and don't feel defeated because it's no longer in alphabetical order. There is still time to find Justine's number even if you have to go through every card. You have to seek before you find. There is a phone number written in your own handwriting back when you were healthy—in large, robust handwriting that also shows her address and work number. You look at your clock and then back at the phone and then call her home phone only to find out it's been disconnected. You close your eyes and remember how she helped you make some meals for your son, even went shopping for him a few times. She was very devoted to you, but you managed to drive her away and so there'd been no contact at all for several years until you sent her the check a couple years ago. But now you've lost her address, and even if you found it, there's no way of knowing if she's still there. Don't think of the ways you hurt Justine—just make the call—if you can find her number—you've done it before.

At her job they say she isn't due in until two days from now. After you hang up you feel better and sit down and write out the check and put it in a stamped envelope which you know now you'll fill out as soon as you call her. Don't think of how this potential act of kindness is due to your son, again. It's too much of a burden to place on him. You need to concentrate more on helping *him*. The last time you were together you thought you saw a secret look of sadness in him as he watched you slowly get up from your couch. He's never asked you about your health, but the expression on his face less than an hour later when you told him about your doctor's appointment to treat your lower back and legs alarmed you.

"I'm feeling a little better since I've been seeing him," you added.

"Good, maybe soon you'll stop limping around like a Wad," he said.

You forced yourself to laugh, but you were also hurt a little. You had probably wanted some sympathy like your mother always wanted sympathy from you but then you realized his remark was just a way to stop talking about anything painful. You also know that you call each other "Wads" as a term of endearment. Fathers can't call their sons "darling" or vice versa, after all. Not past the age of four or five—just accept it, for once. It's like his bouncing the ball, which he does at night in his room for up to a half hour at a time even though he has no interest in sports. Don't worry about what it means—accept the mystery for once. Why did you mistreat Justine, why did your mother mistreat you, why did she make you judge a height contest between her and every girlfriend you ever mistakenly brought home to meet her at her condo in Florida, from when you were eighteen till well after your father died? No one really knows—there are many explanations, many theories, but no real knowledge. It's the same kind of mystery as why you didn't study music with your father, with whom you so rarely fought. Did you think that neither your father nor your mother wanted you to become a musician and compete with them, and so you unconsciously sabotaged yourself to please them? Every child becomes a detective investigating his family. But for once embrace the mystery and stop trying to solve it. That's what your son tells you, in essence, when you start talking about how the universe started. Generally you respect his wishes, although the day he made the "limping like a Wad" comment you might have felt he owed you one and you told him that you thought our solar system was created by God but then abandoned. "Otherwise, we wouldn't be free, Gofus, we'd just be the playthings of God."

"God left to create other worlds," he said.

"Could be, Gofus," you answered.

Somehow the minutes pass. You putter about your condo trying to make it look a little better. Unlike his mother, you are bereft of domestic skills. When you make his bed, you have to lie down in it to tuck the coverlet in. You've given him a nice, large room (a room bigger than yours), but you've done nothing to decorate the walls. There's nothing on those white walls, which look like banks of snow. Justine used to occasionally bring you plants or flowers for other parts of the condo, but your son said he didn't want any for his room. His window looks out on a big magnolia tree that shades it but he always closes the venetian blinds as soon as he is alone in his room.

Before your move, when you and he and his mother all lived in a suburb of Philadelphia and you had to bike a few miles to visit him at his mother's, you always brought a new toy for him. A ball, a children's book, a new *Thomas & Friends* train, some extra tracks for the train setups he used to love to build, etc. Now all the trains are in his big closet, filling almost every inch of space. He never plays with them or appears to ever open his closet. It's as if he's setting an example for you to close the door on your past. The only toy he uses is a small red rubber ball—the one he still bounces so repetitively and then puts away on a miniature shelf. (It struck you recently that it's the same color red as the ball you used to play with when you were a kid.) What he does do during the vast majority of time he spends in his room is sit at his desk, which he keeps pristinely clean, and Google on his laptop or look at his big globe of the world next to which are a stack of different maps, many of which he made himself. But your day always begins with a discussion about things he Googles and then the story. And in thirteen minutes you will do this again, assuming he comes on time.

· · · · ·

It was a magical day, a day of an extended story centered around Garret J. Gunderhold (born Aaron Wadimer), your son's favorite villain. Gunderhold was the headmaster of Wadimer Academy in Wadova before he broke bad, assumed a different name and identity, and built a financial empire from his frighteningly gory amusement parks, as well as from the horror and slasher films he produced, including *Fear Me* and *Fear Me II*. Not satisfied with conquering the entertainment world, he eventually recruited a private army that waged wars, allowing him to be the founder and king of Urge and then to annex other smaller Crasian countries and territories, which he taxed to the hilt. Gunderhold has been your son's favorite character for over two years now while other characters and kingdoms have come and gone. When you sometimes try to revive a character from one of your old stories he gets annoyed or pretends he doesn't remember them. Your stories are not histories. They only function in the present as you tell them, and you never write them down. Once a character ceases to exist in the story he can never come back. In that way, the stories are a kind of metaphor for life. But don't think of that.

It was a wondrous day. There was so much laughter from both of you. You watched him running and even managed to play catch with him in the backyard for a few minutes. You remember thinking how happy you were while you were playing catch. Then you remembered a cab driver who told you his son had Asperger's and how he said to him, "I want to be your friend, just not your only friend." Your son is far too sweet and funny and smart not to make friends eventually, you tell yourself. It will happen.

When his mother came for him the next morning he looked at you a little nervously and said, "Well, goodbye, Wad." You stood by the window and watched him get in the car. You watched the car drive away and kept watching the street for a few seconds more.

. . . . .

When your son doesn't stay overnight, you often have more trouble sleeping. Some of it is because you're alone, and as it grows later and later you think about the people you've lost, like your father or some of your old girlfriends, and you see with such shocking clarity what could have been done so easily to make things better, but some fear or other always interfered. The later it gets the more tormented you are by these thoughts. Eventually, though it gives you disturbing dreams, you take some medication. You feel like you have no alternative except a sleepless night.

It's odd. When you were much younger and a devoted reader of Freud you used to write down your dreams in a notebook you kept by your bed. You tried to remember all your dreams and then free associate with every detail of them you could retrieve. Now you try not to remember, you write nothing down, and you try not to dream, although it's only in your dreams that you're young and can walk and run as you always could. You can even play basketball again. Who was it who called sleep "a little death"? Shakespeare? You know he said "All the world's a stage," and if that's so, then sleeping is a nightly rehearsal to finally die. No wonder some of us have such trouble closing our eyes. We don't want to see our homes again, even if they're castles, we don't want to see our parents—well, we do and we don't.

Lately, you notice that when your son gets excited he talks very fast and sometimes talks over you as your mother once did. You've been wondering if you should bring this up to him, but don't think of it now while you're trying to sleep.

Finally, you begin to relax, finding a position where the pain in your legs is tolerable, and then you are ready, at last, to turn off the television and try to sleep, but no sooner do you close your eyes then you get up in a start and turn on your bed table lamp. On a pad of paper beside your pen you write the words "Call Justine" to remind yourself that she'll be working at the florist tomorrow and that you need to call her to find out her current address.

That last night you did have a dream that you later remembered. You were once again walking in the snow. At first you weren't aware of where you were, then you discovered that you were walking in the mountains. Everywhere you looked there was snow. It's probably true that, like people, no two snowflakes are exactly alike, but it's also true that all snowflakes eventually melt.

In the morning, you and your son continued the story of the master empire builder and career criminal Garret J. Gunderhold, whose latest trick to bolster his country is a series of TV ads in which he promises a job to any immigrant who wants one. "Come to Urge and get a job," he proclaims in one ad. He's also trying to improve the image of his not-so-cryptic dictatorship by creating the Gunder Games as a kind of Urge alternative to the Olympics. Also, he's promoting Gunderhold University with a special offer: "Attend for three years, get the fourth one free." Finally, he's creating yet another national lottery; the winner gets to dine with King Gunderhold in the royal palace. Many other things Gunderholdian were discussed, including Gunderhold's persecution of religious and ethnic minorities like the Gooseists, who believe in interspecies communication and reincarnation and are the special object of Gunderhold's wrath. (His preferred religion is that of the ancient Egyptians, who believed their king was also "Ra," the sun god.)

Don't think of how your son ran and jumped and laughed out loud. It makes you miss him too much.

After his mother took him, you paced around your condominium and wound up in his room. You sat down on his bed and began thinking about your mother and the poodle she trained to never leave her. Then you thought of all the years your father lived alone after his first short marriage before he married your mother. And then you thought of your sister who's never lived with anyone after she left home. There is something about your family with its legacy of loneliness that you find nearly unbearable to think about. But don't think of it. Stick to your plan, instead, of calling Justine. It's 10:45 a.m. now, and she's undoubtedly already in her store.

·　·　·　·　·

You were not in the best of moods when you finally called Justine, but you were hopeful. At least you are finally doing a good thing, you said to yourself. But from her first words you sensed real trouble. It was not merely a sad voice; you'd heard that before, from your sister, for example, before she got on antidepressants. But Justine's voice was beyond sad; it was bleak and blank, like a Holocaust victim's perhaps. You could scarcely bring yourself to ask her how she was—it seemed superfluous. You don't even remember what you said, not even one of your words, only a few of hers. There had been a terrible accident while her youngest son was skiing in Vermont, a freakish collision with a tree, and he had died almost instantly.

You didn't remember any of the details beyond that. It may be that she didn't give you any. There was a lot of silence and very few words and the words themselves were instantly buried like water under ice. You didn't know what to say or do, whether to stay on the phone consoling the inconsolable or to get off and leave her to work with her plants. Somehow in a few minutes the conversation ended. It was like talking with death. The worst thing in the world had happened to Justine, and there was nothing you could say or do. It was only several minutes later that you realized you'd forgotten to ask her address, which was your whole purpose in calling her.

Don't think of her voice. It was like talking to the saddest flute in the world. And this was the person you mistreated more than anyone else and now you couldn't send her the money, at least not for a day or two. As if money could matter to her now anyway.

Immediately you go into your son's room. The maps, the drawings, even his computer—you want to be among them. You want to put your arms around him, but you won't see him for forty-eight hours. You sit down on his bed and think about Justine again—how her eyes glowed when she talked about her boys. Why do we never see the full beauty of people when they are still with us? Don't think of it or of infinity ever again. It's enough that it's true, we shouldn't have to think about it as well, and yet you tried to make people see what you saw, you wanted them to adopt your metaphysics. How selfishly cruel of you. Eliot was right; humankind cannot bear very much reality. Neither can you, you say to yourself. You are a human being, too, no different really than Justine. You've become obsessed with infinity and our permanent inability to understand the universe, and Justine isn't obsessed with that and probably never was, but she's entered a world of shock and grief because of her son's death, and if your son died you would enter the same world and moreover you would certainly end your life. In fact, if you had to experience your son's death, you wouldn't even attempt to live a day longer. Justine is living through your greatest fear and you procrastinated and didn't even have the awareness to ask her for her address.

Don't think of Justine, her tears, her bowed head, the expression on her face she will always live with. Don't think of her voice on the phone, her hello from hell.

You are able to stop thinking about her for a while but only by thinking of the current condition of some of your friends, mostly friends you haven't seen in recent years. Two of your male friends have Parkinson's, one female friend has uterine cancer, another has breast cancer. Then you think of your sister's diabetes, then how your father died of a stroke, how you stood by his bed and watched him in his coma, his body crisscrossed with tubes. Then you think of your mother and her last years with dementia before she, too, died. She thought you were her husband, she thought the chair she sat in was a moving car. And now your sister and you are both limping around, pain in your legs every day.

It's a good thing we have so many aches and pains as we get older or it would be too difficult to face the end. It's selfish, in a way, to love a world where there is so much suffering. But don't think of that. Think of your son's laughter, his running up and down the hallway. Think of him snapping his fingers when he thinks no one can hear him, think of the love in his eyes.

Think of all of this as long as you can.

Of Course He Wanted
to Be Remembered

"Of course he wanted to be remembered, more than anything. He would have loved this."

"What do you mean, 'this'?" Daneen said, quickly adjusting her dark-rimmed glasses.

"What we're doing now, man," Margo said. "Remembering him over a cup of coffee in Starbucks. How perfect!"

"Yet he didn't ultimately even believe in memory."

Margo played with a couple of curls in her newly colored reddish-blond hair as if stalling for time. "I have to say I don't really know what you mean by that."

Daneen looked at her almost sternly.

"OK. Remember his 'your memory is your fiction' lectures? His belief that memory has no objective basis in reality?"

"That sounds like him."

"Remember his saying, 'Personal memory is the first casualty of infinity. Cultural memory is the second'?"

"He was always so grandiose."

"He said what he thought, and he happened to think that. I don't know—does that make him grandiose? To me he was an artist more than he was a philosopher, anyway. He was able to communicate so much."

"You really think he was an artist? I mean, in any kind of important way?"

"Of course. His poetry, his paintings."

"Really? You didn't see a kind of amateurish quality, especially in the paintings, which I think are flat-out academic, honestly?"

"I think his teaching was his greatest art form," Daneen said. "It just happened to take place in a classroom instead of a gallery or museum."

Margo nodded perfunctorily.

Daneen waited for her to say something, but she didn't. "You seem...I don't know...disappointed," she said.

"Disappointed? What do you mean, disappointed? You've got to elaborate on that, girlfriend."

Daneen's eyes opened wide, then blinked rapidly a few times in succession.

"I don't know—you seem almost angry whenever I praise Peter, even though we're meeting to memorialize him, or so I thought."

"I thought we met to, like, share our memories, not just our tributes," Margo said, finally looking in her direction, Daneen thought.

"But all your memories of him seem to be disappointments. You do nothing but criticize him."

"Girlfriend, I criticized some aspects of his work and some aspects of his thinking but I haven't said a word against Peter as a man. At least, I didn't mean to."

"I guess I didn't know him personally as well as you did, so I just admire what I do know from him as my teacher."

"Really? It's surprising that you would say that."

Their order was ready, and Daneen jumped up from her chair to get the mocha lattes (a type of coffee she would never drink alone), clearly grateful to leave the table for a moment. Margo, meanwhile, moved her chair back a little, stretched out, and even spread her legs a bit—a gesture that used to be considered unladylike, Daneen thought. Margo was always flaunting her unselfconsciousness because she knew she was pretty enough to get away with it.

"Here's the coffee," Daneen said.

"Thanks. Wow, it's hot."

Daneen nodded. She was looking out the window at the people of St. Louis passing by. It was her turn to act a little distracted, she figured, hoping that Margo noticed, but Margo waited patiently until they made eye contact before speaking again.

"So, listen, I wanted to say that I think Peter was an absolutely extraordinary person who transformed my life in many ways, and I really thought it was obvious that I feel that way. I mean we talk about Peter whenever we see each other, which, granted, isn't that often, but which certainly is more than this, like, once a year 'memorial,' if you want to call it that. I mean we do get together, what would you say, a half-dozen times a year?"

"It's more like four. Three or four."

"Three seems a little low, but even if it is three, that's still three times more than once."

Daneen forced a little laugh, then looked around at the other customers, people of all ages, if not all races. It was like the room was an exhibit in a museum illustrating the different stages of white life. Then Margo finally spoke.

"So, I was surprised when you said a little while ago that you didn't know Peter as well as I did."

"Yes. I meant outside of class."

"Yeah, I find it strange that you'd say that when you seemed to see him almost every day—either in his office, or in the cafeteria. And I know you proofread his last book, which he even acknowledged in the book with a very cool tribute, so I'm sure you had a lot of contact with him about that."

"I'm not saying that I didn't know him personally, just that it wasn't on the level that you knew him."

"Meaning?"

"Meaning, I didn't have an affair with him and you did, didn't you? I mean, I think you even told me once on the phone."

"Well, girlfriend, didn't you sleep with him, too? I mean, at least once, anyway?"

Daneen touched her glasses again, then shook her head. "Uh-uh," she said. "Didn't happen."

"Not even once?"

"No, never happened."

"Not even once?"

"You look shocked," Daneen said.

Margo's hands went back to fiddling rapidly with her hair as if she were playing a fast riff on a guitar.

"I wouldn't say shocked. If you told me that my father just died, I'd be shocked, even though he had his second heart attack less than two months ago. That would be shocking to me."

"God, I'm so sorry. I didn't know," Daneen said, putting her hand over her mouth as if she'd unwittingly announced the news.

Margo looked up. "Thanks," she said. "I didn't mean to shock you with my shock and set off a chain reaction of shocks here. It was just an example."

"The thousand natural shocks / That flesh is heir to," Daneen said. "That was one of Peter's favorite lines from Shakespeare."

"Yeah, man, I know."

"Of course…Anyway, that's horrible about your father. I didn't know."

"Well, things are much better now. More, like, stabilized for the moment."

"Good. Great."

"So, no need to talk about it anymore."

Daneen looked at Margo closely. "I'm sorry I jumped all over you about what you said about Peter. I way overreacted."

"No worries," Margo said, making a dismissive gesture with her hand and in the process causing Daneen to notice the stylish gold bracelet she wore around her right wrist. Margo always looked stylish no matter how much she touted her "ghetto" background (she was half Hispanic). Daneen could never dress as well as Margo or, why not admit it, look half as hot, either.

"And I'm sorry for what I said about you and Peter sleeping together. Completely uncalled for, whether you were or weren't. And, of course, now I know you weren't."

Daneen nodded, forcing a smile.

"Not that it would have mattered to me either way, obviously, since I assumed all this time that you had."

"But why did you assume that?"

"I didn't assume it; I thought it."

"You said 'assumed it.' "

"Okay, maybe I assumed it because you talked about him so much and spent so much time with him. I'm pretty sure you spent more time with him than I did."

"So you assumed that's what we were doing even though you knew I knew he was married and also knew, part of the time, he was involved with you, my *friend*? You really think that of me?"

No, I don't think you have the guts, Margo thought, but instead quickly said, "A., He'd been estranged from his wife for almost two years, which I did assume you knew, and B., I didn't think we were really close friends then."

"We were friends then."

"Not close."

"What were we then?"

"Basically classmates, very intrigued by the same professor, who got together every now and then to talk, mostly about his ideas, which we both found...fascinating, I guess."

"They *were* fascinating. Or did they lose their juice, for you, over time?"

"Juice?"

"Impact."

Margo nodded then turned away for a moment. "I still think they are fascinating, some of them. I never said they weren't."

"You said his painting was academic and dull."

"Painting isn't the same thing as ideas, is it?"

Daneen stared blankly at Margo. She would never be as smart as Margo, she thought, though she was a better student, GPA-wise. She knew she had read many more books than Margo, but Margo was street smart, people smart, maybe even life smart, though for some reason, she tried to hide it.

"But, girlfriend, I do still feel some of Peter's ideas *are* fascinating," Margo said. "I mean, I can find them interesting without agreeing with them, right? Just like I can find reading about the effects of mescaline or even heroin fascinating, but that doesn't mean I intend to ever take them...again."

"I get it. I concede the point."

"I mean, I don't mean to come off as if I'm, like, debating you or whatever."

Daneen shrugged. "Even if you were, Peter loved debates.

Those were some of our best classes, when we got into a good class debate. Don't you agree with that?"

"Peter loved debates as long as they were about his own ideas...but nothing wrong with that," Margo added quickly.

· · · · ·

Strange the way time could gather and then so rapidly disappear, like thin clouds blowing across the sky so fast you could barely identify them. Strange, too, how you could be so quickly transported to another place, as Daneen had been now to Margo's apartment, which she'd seen briefly—for just a few minutes a couple of times—but where she was now leisurely sipping vodka, clutching the notebook that she'd brought to Starbucks on Margo's orange sofa (Margo loved loud colors, but somehow made them work), and answering a question about her fellowship when it was now past ten-thirty already. It felt like they'd been together for days.

"All it means is that I'm prolonging being a student for another year or so."

"Hey, don't demean it. It's still an awesome honor, man. So, what is it exactly that you have to do for it?" Margo said. She was sitting on a bright orange throw rug, occasionally resting her drink on a long glass table between them. Everything looked a little too expensive for Margo, who had only recently ceased being a student and now was a hostess at a mid-level Italian restaurant on the Hill. Daneen guessed she could pass for Italian, too.

Daneen looked down at the table. "So it involves a little teaching, but the main thing I have to do is show some substantial progress on a book."

"A book!" Margo blurted. "Really? How cool! What kind of book will it be?"

26

Daneen reddened. "Oh, nonfiction. I'm not exactly Jane Austen."

"So then, will it be, like, criticism?"

"It'll be more like a critical biography. I'm writing about Peter, actually."

Oh, then it will be an uncritical biography, Margo thought, deciding to keep the joke to herself. "Yours will be the first one, then."

"I hope so."

"That's cool."

"Thank you. I was actually hoping we could talk some more about him, if you don't mind, sometime in the fairly near future, for the book."

"How candid do you want this book to be?"

Daneen looked puzzled, which made her seem, Margo thought, at least five years younger than she was. It was disarming, but it could be irritating, too.

"I mean, will you want me to talk about my relationship or what?"

Daneen's face reddened even more now, making her look still younger. "Oh, no, nothing like that."

"It will be more of an academic book, then?"

"I don't know. I don't know what kind of book it will be," Daneen said, getting up from the sofa to pace a little, as she often did.

Margo fixed herself another drink. Daneen couldn't live in denial indefinitely, could she? Margo thought. You couldn't write a book, take money for writing a book, and then construct a fantasy life the book's subject never lived, could you? Well, you could, but it would be wrong on every level. Was that how Daneen wanted to begin her adult life? Although Margo couldn't really picture her as a true adult. She still saw her in the future as a wide-eyed—albeit academically precocious—child babbling worshipfully about her male idols of the moment like an acolyte refusing to see the truth about her god. And there would be others after Peter who Daneen would turn into deities not because she actually knew them but because she had the need to create them, Margo was sure of that.

She finished her drink and put it back on the glass table. Daneen was staring at her.

"What?" Margo finally said.

"Maybe you should tell me now."

"What about?"

"About your relationship with Peter so I can figure out how to put it in the book."

"I thought you didn't want stuff like that."

"I'm not sure what I want...in the book, but I think I should hear about it anyway. I mean, don't you think it makes more sense to gather as much material as I can first and then start deciding what to winnow out and what to include? Peter used to say 'The writer gathers first then throws a potlatch.' "

"Makes sense to me," Margo said, starting to sip another drink, although she already felt somewhat tipsy. She stumbled, spilling a little liquor, before resuming her place on the rug.

"So," Daneen said, adjusting her glasses, "you want to just sorta tell me, or whatever?"

"It was probably very much the way you'd imagine it," Margo blurted. "At first, anyway. Me, the adoring schoolgirl hanging on his every word," she said, reminding herself to edit the story a bit since Daneen still was essentially an "adoring schoolgirl," herself.

"We all hung on his every word."

"Yeah, but I started visiting him a lot in his office."

"A lot of us did that, too."

"So, yeah, girlfriend, a lot of us did that, too, but a lot of us weren't from my background, shall we say, so it kind of blew me away, given where I came from and being Hispanic."

"That's true," Daneen said softly, possibly to herself, but probably not loud enough to be heard, in any case.

"So, when he started to touch me in his office, man, you know, I was pretty defenseless. I knew I wasn't his first student so I wasn't *that* freaked out, but Peter was a world-class worrier despite all his brave 'seize the day'–type language in class. He didn't want to jeopardize his position at the university. He loved that more than anything."

"He loved his art," Daneen said from the sofa, staring at her intently, like some kind of night watchman.

"He loved his art, and he would have loved getting famous for it even more, but fame, outside the school, was something he always chased after but never really got. In the school he was famous, but he was only a *college* legend. Who knows, maybe that's why he slept with his students: to make up for not being famous enough."

"He slept with *some* of his students, a very few of them, I think."

"Over the years, I'm pretty sure it was more than a few. Anyway, he was very careful and worried all the time and made me swear all kinds of oaths not to tell anyone, which I didn't for the first week or so. And I didn't tell *any* people, really, only those few who I thought had good judgment."

"Where did you meet?" Daneen said, looking down to the right of Margo at the bright corner of the rug.

"Well, his wife was home a lot then."

"Bedridden, I heard."

"Something like that. I didn't ask, much, and he definitely didn't want to talk about it. Anyway, we mostly met in my apartment and sometimes went to a motel. And, you know, in the beginning it was pretty exciting."

"What would ever make it not exciting?"

Margo laughed ironically. "When you find out he's doing other people besides you."

Daneen redirected her eyes to Margo's face, as if they were tennis balls she'd just hit hard in her direction.

"He told you this?"

"Do men ever tell?"

"I don't know...sometimes...did you walk in and see it?"

"No, but look, the important thing is that I *knew*...You look skeptical, but don't you believe that if I *say* I knew, that I'd know something like that?"

"I don't believe in secondhand information, especially about something like that."

"One of the girls he did it with told me herself. He was cheating on both of us at the same time. I'll admit he was a smart dude and somehow kept his looks, more or less, to the end—probably with the help of a lot of good face work, but face facts, he was a complete pussy hound. Sorry, there's no other way to put it—and the dude blamed it all on his parents. Remember his saying 'You can't save others if you've already been robbed by them'? As usual, he was really pitying himself if you listened closely enough."

"So did you ever confront him about it?"

"I was a kid, so no, not really. Should have, though."

Daneen smiled ambiguously, then bent down and withdrew her notebook from her absurdly oversized pocketbook and began reading: "The secrets of man are so trivial they're hardly worth mentioning."

"What's that?" Margo said, pointing to the notebook.

"It's a collection of some things Peter wrote or said in class."

"Quotations from Chairman Peter, huh?"

"Listen," she said, reading from the notebook again. "This came from our class: 'In the absence of things we invent them. Hence the invention of God.' "

"But he did believe in God, or powers greater than us. He just didn't think we knew anything about them. He was adamant about that. It was one of the few things he ever talked about with me besides his sexual fantasies, so I remembered."

"Well, I know what I heard. That came from one of his classes. Maybe he said it to you, too."

"He probably said 'God' instead of 'religion' because it sounded more dramatic or more musical," Margo said. "It was drama that he really loved, not philosophy."

"You're obviously skeptical, but believe me, I took copious notes, and he said it in class."

"Yes, copious notes, and now you'll have a copious book."

Daneen shut her notebook, which made a sharp sound. "Is that bad?"

"What?"

"Do you resent my book?"

"Resent it? Why would I?"

"Just that anyone would love…Peter's work enough to write a book about him."

"I thought the book was about his life."

"His work *was* his life."

"Tell that to his wife and all his lovers. I think Peter's mother—who he pretty much blamed for how he treated women, except when he blamed his father—was more important to him than Schopenhauer, Nietzsche, and Wittgenstein put together."

Daneen got up from her sofa. "Well, OK, you've made yourself clear. I think I should probably go now."

Margo stood up, too. "So you don't intend your book to include anyone who had a less than adoring view of him, do you, girlfriend? It's going to be more of a heroic biography than a critical one, isn't it?"

"That's an unfair thing to say. Pretty cruel, actually."

" 'The truth on first hearing is often cruel and is rejected like music we can't initially understand.' Another saying from your guru."

Daneen clutched her notebook like she were strangling it, Margo thought. It was as if, her mind having temporarily failed, Daneen's body spontaneously rose to her defense with a sudden explosion of her most intense redness yet. She clutched her bag preternaturally tight.

Daneen turned around then and started walking until she reached the door. Then she turned again and faced Margo, who'd been following her.

"OK, Margo, here's your last chance to tell me how awful he was. I promise I'll put whatever you say in the book."

"You just don't get it, do you? I don't want to hurt any of his fans or admirers, least of all you. That definitely ain't my goal."

"What is your goal then?"

"I thought it was understood we were meeting to talk about Peter, you and me. You know, a free conversation. I didn't know anything about your damn book."

"So you say one thing and then you say another. I mean, why

don't you just tell me, book or no book, what exactly he did to you that was so evil?"

"I never said evil. I don't believe in evil, really, except with people like the Nazis or whatever."

"What did he do then that was so disappointing to you that you've become this bitter about the man who was your lover, for God's sake?"

"You don't really want to know."

"No. I do want to know. I actually do."

Margo looked hard at her. "You don't expect me to give you all the details, do you?"

"Give me what you can."

"I was kind of innocent then, you know, no matter how I dressed or what you heard. I mean, I know people ran their mouths about me, and I wasn't exactly a virgin, but I was still kind of innocent, and he took me to some pretty dark places... So, you want, like, the specifics?"

"So you mean like threesomes, that kind of thing? I heard he did that."

"No, he was too scared to have witnesses, but other things, definitely."

"So, drugs?"

"I always felt I had to take whatever drug he gave me. You know, the last years he was a complete addict. Heroin, too."

"So, was he abusive to you?"

"You'd have to define what abusive means."

"Did he hurt you physically without your consent?"

Margo looked away.

"Sometimes, he'd just do something I thought was outrageous, and I'd just go along with it. It was my misguided attempt to seem sophisticated, and meanwhile he could feed off my youth like a vampire whenever he needed a fix. Youth—just having a few moments of it was his true drug, and the more he needed it the more desperate things he'd do to get just a second of it," Margo said, her eyes glistening.

"Do you think he was so different from other people that way?"

"No, of course not."

"Don't you think his health had something to do with it, too?"

"Sure, probably."

"And don't you think women are like that, too?" Daneen said, trying to keep her voice controlled.

"Aging is a bitch, no question."

"A tragedy."

"A bitch. But there are different ways of handling it. I mean he took a very destructive path to get his youth fix, and he used some innocent people along the way."

"Why do you call it 'using'?" Daneen said. "Everyone who he chose to know he cared about."

"You say this based on what?"

"He listened to people, really listened to them. He listened to me like no one ever had, least of all my parents. He listened to people's dreams."

"Yeah, man, I know. He listened to mine, too, but then he'd use what he heard to get more power over people, and their dreams never really came true."

"So, you can't expect him to listen to everyone's dreams and make them all come true, can you? And by the way, he didn't try to get power over me, ever. Not even once."

"Sorry. I shouldn't have said that."

"Toward the end he was very sick and his conduct slipped a

little, I'll admit that," Daneen said. "I'm sure if he were alive now, he'd feel very badly about it."

"He had his cross to bear," Margo said. "His wife had MS for seven years or something."

"Give him credit for taking care of her, then, even while he was maybe losing it a little. I mean, his wife dying, his mother's death, and then his cancer."

"The man did some good things, no doubt, but he always put his own needs first. He pretended he didn't, but he was faithful to no one. Sorry, I can't forgive him for that yet, not completely."

Daneen meant to nod but instead looked at her watch. "Margo, it's getting really late. I should probably go now."

"Yes, of course, I get it."

"Maybe another time we can talk," she said, looking past her, Margo thought, as if at something startling, like a sudden rainbow.

"Sure, another time," Margo said.

· · · · ·

It was like a bath of blood. Like the first time she had a period in her bathtub and saw the water slowly redden. Now, she suddenly saw red everywhere. In the stoplight on Hanley Street and on the flag in front of Manhattan Café, where her car was parked. Red lipstick on the women walking in the Central West End. Red or a color like red that she wasn't cool enough to know, though Margo would. And it all seemed to be coming from her red face—Daneen the queen of red, the color of shame and rage and, in Margo's case, the color of her red sex with Peter.

She sank into her bed as into a tomb, a kind of motel tomb, which was always waiting for her, with a vacancy for her alone. At least when she closed her eyes now the redness went away. She saw instead the baby blue of Peter's eyes on the late afternoon when she went to his office—sad, empathetic, oddly innocent eyes, not the dark eyes of the worldly Margo (who, Daneen suspected, greatly exaggerated the "trauma" of her past).

That innocence, so strange in an older man, was something Margo could never see, no matter how many times she had sex with him and despite what their sex was really like.

Yet she, Daneen, had gone to his office that day in the hopes of having that kind of red sex. She'd hemmed and hawed and even stuttered, she was so scared, but she could stand it no longer—she had loved him for at least two years, and taken all of his classes, plus an independent study. She was a senior then and wanted to lose her virginity to him. Who else? The boys at her college were boys, as her father had warned her, but Peter had not only lived, he'd lived a significant life.

He looked at her, understanding what she couldn't express coherently, and responded with a hug that she wished she could disappear into so it would never end. But when it did end she had to face the cold fact that it wasn't going to happen because he didn't want it to. He was so inventively protective of her in his excuses—she could still remember them all. He quickly cited deep concern for his mother's health and the fact that, though separated, he and his wife still weren't divorced. Finally, he mentioned the enormous pressure he was under because his department, his school "that I've given my life to, has turned against me and is trying to take away my tenure. Discovering us like this would be the cherry on their sundae of death for me."

"But you're worth more than the whole rest of the university put together," Daneen blurted.

"Thank you, dearest Daneen."

"Is there anything I can do to help? Petitions? Protests? I'd gladly organize them. Very gladly. It would be an honor."

"They'd think that I told you and the other students to do it. To work, there'd have to be massive protests. They'd have to appear spontaneous yet be massive. The media outside the school would have to cover them, too."

"I can do it; I know I can."

"I don't know."

"We have to do something."

They hugged again, her breasts pressing slightly against him, and he said, "Dearest Daneen, you've always been my favorite student and my most faithful one, and I'll always love you in the deepest part of my heart."

She cried a little but there was no red sex, no sex at all. Three days later she found out Peter was sleeping with Margo.

There were wars, famines, and tsunamis going on in the world but Daneen, despite her normally high level of social commitment, threw herself into her Save Peter movement for the next two weeks (in spite of what she'd learned about Margo) with a frenzied devotion she'd never felt before. But after three well-attended campus rallies, two of them covered by local TV, Peter resigned. They'd come up with new evidence involving not only sex with other students but also drugs he'd taken with his students—and not just pot but cocaine, even mescaline. The university moved with uncharacteristic swiftness while Peter lawyered up as best he could. Finally, a settlement was reached. He was formally censured and was forced to resign with a year's severance pay. It was around then that he admitted he had colon cancer—a classic case of a man being afraid for too long to see a doctor.

Daneen had always partially suspected that Margo had ratted him out one way or another about the drugs and probably the sex, too. She was a chronic braggart who couldn't help herself, and Peter was her most impressive trophy male to date. He was so handsome then, and he stayed that way right until almost the end. But until tonight, she'd had no proof that Margo had turned on him. When she thought about it, as she was now in her motel tomb, it made her so mad she became red again.

• • • • •

Margo was cooling out in her bathtub—after the day she'd had, she deserved to just lie back in the warmth and listen to the music from the next room, a kind of pop/jazz Peter the purist would never approve of. She saw an image of his worried, fixated eyes—Peter and his mad quest for women. And women were so foolish (herself included). Why did they seek the bodies of men so frenetically when water so often made them feel better? Peter always was so concerned that she feel "good" during sex, that she come as if answering a question on a test, but Professor Peter supposedly didn't believe in tests. He should have cooled out like the water and just been there for her.

She finished the joint she was smoking, tossed it into the sink. She was well coordinated, had played high school volleyball and basketball. It helped her get a scholarship. She was so good at so many things—why didn't he see that? He lorded his supposed worldliness over her, spending his wife's money, no doubt, to see half the world, then, when the scandal hit, he cried like a baby. Couldn't he see how her youth was an advantage in life? At least in the real world—not that he'd ever know it. She came from the working class. He from Newport Beach money in Rhode Island. She knew about real people. He never did.

She closed her eyes, wanting to get back to a peaceful place again in the water. Daneen was like fire—the opposite of water. She felt like she'd been at war with Daneen all day. There was a time when she wanted to be friends with Daneen, when she admired her intellectual passion and idealism (something she could never have), but now she saw how futile Daneen was, too. She was terminally naïve, too protected by endless illusions. How could she understand Margo, who had to work for everything she got—not to mention dealing with a date rape or two along the way. Daneen was a terminally wealthy WASP through and through. No chance for understanding there. If she knew about the money Peter had lent her near the end, she'd probably misunderstand and call her a whore, in her mind anyway.

At least Peter was open-minded about sex and other things, too—had even given Margo an A when she'd only asked for a B+ to keep her scholarship. Had written her a great recommendation, too.

It was odd how people had so many different sides to them. She remembered one day before they were lovers, before any of the trouble at school started, when they had a great talk in the college snack bar about books, teaching, and her future. As they walked out of the snack bar down the hall toward the school parking lot, he told her he'd been diagnosed with colon cancer. Her eyes immediately teared, and he said, "Not to worry. Cancer has no chance of beating me." He opened the door—it was raining steadily. "Know why?"

She was too stunned to say anything.

" 'Cause I love life too much—I finally figured that out."

Then he opened his umbrella and sheltered her from the rain.

Uncle Ray

LITTLE DID you know then, when you first stood alone on its white wooden raft, lord of the lake you looked out upon, how many times you would return to it as you have again today. You loved so many things about the Berkshires but none more than you loved the lake, just as you loved so many things about the lake but nothing more than when you were a kid and played King of the Raft with your summer friends. And then when the kids left to go eat their suppers and you were alone on the raft, as you are now, all these years later, you could stand with your hands on your hips once again, however briefly the raft's absolute ruler.

Lake Mahkeenac is surrounded by green hills. Looking left to right, you can see part of Beachwood, then the mysterious, much-storied little island you rowed out to several times, once with a girl. Then, a couple miles beyond that, the red-brick monastery at the base of the hill, then below that, Tanglewood beach. To the right of the beach are the cottages of Mahkeenac Shores that eventually lead to the Stockbridge Town Beach, just a five-minute walk from Beachwood. There was a green wooden snack shop there where you could buy Creamsicles, hot dogs, and root beer. There were always chips in the green-painted wood of the snack bar and holes in the screened windows, which several flies inevitably penetrated on a daily basis, and the swollen wooden floor always smelled of mustard and damp bathing suits. But you loved it anyway. Sometimes you'd go there with friends and sometimes you'd go alone and occasionally after your snack you'd take a swim at the Stockbridge beach. But always, you eventually returned to Beachwood, where most of your friends were, and played on the raft or later flirted with the Beachwood girls, in the way you did then.

There were also adults at the lake, of course. Some were in the orchestra that played during the summer festival at Tanglewood but most were just homeowners spending part of their summer by the lake. Occasionally, they swam, but mostly they read newspapers and talked in their white wooden chairs on the small, sandy beach below the grove. You were glad when they left, especially when they left the raft so you could play with your friends. Getting thrown into the water, or jumping before you were thrown, always left you laughing faster than you could draw breath, it seemed.

Thinking of that, you turn around on the raft. You were facing the hills but now you look at the beach and see that there's no one there, either adults or children. It's a late afternoon in early June and the music festival won't start for two or three weeks so it's not entirely surprising that you're the only one here. In fact, you don't really want to see anyone you knew who would remember you. It's been over twenty-five years since your last visit. You feel oddly self-conscious in a way to be here when you're simply revisiting one of the sacred haunts of your youth, not staying with anyone or doing anything work-related.

It all happened so simply. You were looking for a place to go on your vacation. One that wouldn't be too expensive but that would take you out of your city life, where you were one among millions, to a place that in some fundamental way identified you. You thought about visiting your parents. Your mother lived in Florida, your father near Philadelphia—but whenever you visited one of them the other would get hurt, and you didn't have the money to visit both. Besides, with either one you had to be hypervigilant to avoid topics that could inevitably lead to arguments either about your job, which didn't pay you enough, or the fact that you still weren't married. You finally realized that to visit either one of them was to risk being ambushed not only by a possible fight in the present but by any one of a number of lurking, only temporarily hidden memories that could suddenly appear and shock you, as if your memory were playing hide-and-seek with you.

Eventually, you thought of writing your brother, who was married and pretty well off and had access to quite the summer house in the Hamptons. He was nicer than he used to be, say, around the time of your parents' divorce, but you didn't get the feeling that he really wanted to see you. It was as if you'd failed him in some unalterably subtle way. He'd be friendly enough in his emails or on the phone, but this surface friendliness hadn't translated into any sort of invitation in over two years. You could only conclude that he disapproved of you in the same quiet way your father did and that your big brother was also disappointed that you hadn't gotten promoted in either your career or your love life. He, too, was waiting for you to get married, as if that alone could finally certify you as an adult or at least allay the fears you sensed that he and your parents might have that you were secretly gay (though they'd never said that, they were wrong-headed and fearful enough to think it).

After eliminating your family, you began to think of your friends, even an ex-girlfriend in one case. But, as they say in football, upon further review there was something wrong about each potential visit. Not the least was the fear that it would trigger a sad series of memories, since in every case you were not as close to those friends with homes in appealing places as you used to be.

You went to bed for the next few nights with your vacation plans unresolved. One night, you had a long and unusually lucid dream that took place in Beachwood, a small community in the Berkshires. In the dream, you were swimming in Lake Mahkeenac near the summer cottage your parents were renting. After a while you swam out to the raft, which you stood on as a king would stand and felt incredibly revitalized.

When you woke up, you were flooded by Berkshires memories, memories of the happiest summers of your life. But would it be potentially painful to revisit? You tried to visualize it—but it didn't scare you. You thought long and hard about it, but concluded that you had finally found your bad-memory-proof place to visit.

· · · · ·

Now you are here, staring at the beach and the grove beyond it, struck by its very emptiness. You never missed a summer in the Berkshires throughout your childhood and into the start of your teens. Unfortunately, your parents always rented, so when they divorced and stopped coming to the Berkshires there was no house that you or your brother could stay in. Also, by then, your brother had already moved to New York. Soon, he started summering at his well-heeled father-in-law's home in East Hampton.

Well, now you're back. It took all these years for you to finally return, but you're glad you did. Now you can once again walk through the maze-like formal gardens at Tanglewood, even though the orchestra won't begin to play for three weeks or so, pass the streets of Lenox, where you used to swim with your brother at the Curtis Hotel's outdoor pool, and eat once more at the Red Lion Inn at Stockbridge, your favorite restaurant, where you had dinner with more than one girlfriend you thought you'd be with forever. Even just walking the sloping roads of the Mahkeenac shores or Mahkeenac Heights where most of your summer pals once lived was a pleasure, albeit a poignant one.

You have been sitting on the raft, dangling your feet in the lake, wondering if your toes will be nibbled by any bluegills, as they used to be, when you suddenly stand up again and look back at the beach and grove. Then you see a tall man in a bathing suit walking along the sand, as if trying to decide which chair to sit on. There's something youthful about the way he walks: he moves with a little too much energy, and yet his hair appears to be mostly gray. He's the type of man who for some reason reminds you of many other men—he has the restless energy of your father, for example, but also that of your boss.

You turn around again, your back to the man, and look out at the lake simply because it's more satisfying to look at the hills than at a man you don't recognize. It seems like the right thing to do, but fifteen seconds later, as if responding to a delayed itch, you turn around and look more closely at him. Then it hits you that the man is most probably Uncle Ray.

He's not your uncle, God knows. That was just his nickname, and no one from Beachwood ever called him anything else. Uncle Ray was a homeowner and year-round resident who lived in a modest red cottage near the grove. He was a lifer, and was even born only twenty miles or so away in North Adams, Massachusetts. Though he wasn't a man of many words, everyone liked him as far as you could tell. For as long as you came to the Berkshires, you remember him always being there like an inevitable part of the scenery. Being shy, though, you didn't talk to him much. He was one of those people whose looks never really change from the way you first saw them. Uncle Ray was tall and lean and clean-shaven with dark brown, fairly short hair, a little longer than a crew cut. You almost always saw him in the grove in his navy blue bathing suit, bare-chested or wearing an open shirt, his muscles fairly well developed, the upper part of his chest partially covered by dark hair. He had a fairly toothy smile, too; his front teeth were often visible when he talked as well. Maybe that's why he didn't speak that often. He loved his motorboat, which was docked at the lake, and would sometimes take a ride in it with a woman friend (he had a number of them) or sometimes with kids from Beachwood. You wanted to ride with him but were afraid to ask, and once when he asked you, you said no. But if he were on the beach or on the raft and your eyes met he would always wave hello. Other than that you only saw him at the grocery store in Lenox once and another time at Hagyard's Pharmacy, where you were licking a vanilla ice cream cone. He waved at you then, too, and you waved back. He seemed to be a pretty cool adult. You didn't know what he did for a living then but one of the big kids on the raft said Ray had once been drafted by the Red Sox and had played a season or two in the minor leagues. You did see him play catch in the grove with a friend of his and lots of times with kids a little older than you and he looked really good so you hoped the part about being in the minor leagues was true. Eventually, you discovered that he worked for some local business doing construction. His cottage was pretty small and you'd heard that he'd inherited it from his parents. You knew that he coached a Little League team for a couple of years, but you can't make a living from that. Anyway, if you owned a home it didn't cost that much to live in the Berkshires then.

You look more closely at the man now as if you're studying an alien you've never seen before. You're thinking that there's at least a 50% chance that it's Uncle Ray and you wonder how it never occurred to you that you might see him during your visit. You feel a kind of queasiness in your chest moving down into your stomach as you remember that day on the raft you were, of course, bound to remember. You're not exactly sure how old you were, either thirteen or just turned fourteen. Had you been fifteen, you would have known what to do much better, just as your brother, who's four years older than you, would have not only known what to do but would have done it right away, almost instinctively. You were a young thirteen.

It was about the same time as it is today, though you think it must have been in the last week in June when the concert season started. You were sitting alone on the raft after reviewing the last disappointing King of the Raft game you'd played earlier that day. Still, you just wanted to stay out on the raft as long as you could: you were upset, and things at home had been tense with your parents lately, especially with your father, who was pushing you to get a part-time job. You kept rotating your position on the raft so that on the one side you could see the hills at the end of the lake and on the other the little beach and the dark-green grove behind it. When you looked at the grove you saw Uncle Ray doing something with his boat. You kept looking at him wondering if he might ask you to play catch or Wiffle ball. Your brother didn't like playing catch or doing much of anything with you anymore, and your father didn't enjoy watching or playing sports. Ditto your mother, who mainly liked sitting by the lake and reading magazines. It was as if your family was emotionally paralyzed, somehow one step removed from humanity, and just when you were so starved for attention you would have welcomed anything from them, even some kind of psychological assault.

Now you remember why you didn't have a good King of the Raft that day. Joey Sneerson, a big kid, had gotten carried away and thrown skinny, bespectacled Peter Schwartz into the water harder than he should have, and also insulted him more than usual.

"Hey, saltpeter, drown like the little worm you are," Joey bellowed, striding across the raft like a lion.

You could see that Peter's face was getting red and that he was very close to crying (perhaps he already had cried a little) and that he was also almost out of breath. You wanted to say something to intervene on his behalf but you were busy treading water because you didn't like how hard Joey threw you into the water either. You remember trying to create a scenario where the two of you could throw Joey off the raft but you couldn't really believe in it. Finally, Joey let Peter swim away as he yelled out, "I'm the King of the Raft, you little vermin!" Meanwhile, you hoped he had forgotten about you. Indeed, less than a minute later, the King must have gotten lonely or hungry or cold (hopefully all three). After cannonballing into the water, he swam to shore himself.

Hidden by the raft and still treading water, you watched him towel off, hating him every second and yourself, too, for not sticking up for Peter. When Joe finally left, you climbed up the raft's little ladder and lay down exhausted. That's when you saw Uncle Ray by his boat. Soon, you started rotating your position, vaguely wondering if he'd ask you to play catch.

Then the next time you looked at him you saw him in his bathing suit diving into the water and watched his long, sleek strokes as if he were a fish. He swam toward you on the raft, which somehow made you feel both nervous and excited. Then he stood near you, as if he were the new Raft King.

"Hey, how's it going?" he said, with his toothy smile. It was the first kind voice you'd heard all day.

You shrugged, feeling fairly close to crying yourself, so you turned your back to him and moved to a far corner of the raft, where you dangled your feet into the water, wondering about the bluegills.

The next thing you knew, Uncle Ray walked across the raft and sat next to you. There he was, Beachwood royalty sitting next to you on the raft!

"Saw you playing King of the Raft out there. Looked like things were getting a little rough."

How did he know what they called it? Had he, too, played your game (that you'd thought you'd invented) when he was a kid? Now you had to hide your astonishment as well as your sadness, so you merely shrugged again.

"That Joe's got a little mean streak in him, doesn't he?"

"I guess."

"He shouldn't throw kids off the raft the way he does. Someone could get hurt."

"I know," you said, turning to look at him for a second. His eyes had changed somehow. They looked softer. You didn't notice his teeth, either.

"Next time he starts acting that way you let me know, and I'll talk to him."

You nodded. It sounded good, but he wasn't always on the beach when Joey was.

"Just say 'Uncle Ray' or wave to me, and I'll swim out and make him stop."

"Thanks," you said softly.

Uncle Ray said nothing for a while, which you took to mean the King of the Raft issue was settled. You remember worrying what you would talk about next. You also had to pee but to do that you'd have to jump in the lake and you thought it might be rude to desert him so soon after he said he'd come to your rescue, so you had to put up with these discomforts, which seemed a small enough price to pay. Meanwhile, it was getting colder and darker and you were due home for supper. (Also, you'd been getting tired of lying to your parents about why you were late, but there was still nothing you could think of to say.)

Finally, Ray turned towards you and said, "Do you like this time of day?"

"Yeah," you said, slightly puzzled by the question.

"It's pretty out, isn't it? I mean the sky and the way the trees look in the grove."

"Yes, it is," you said, stopping short of saying the word "pretty" because your brother had once made fun of you for using it.

"I like to swim here this time of day, do you?"

"Yeah."

"It's nice to be here when everyone's gone, don't you think? When it's quiet and peaceful. Do you feel that way, too?"

"Yes," you said, though you had never really thought about it, since you liked the lake at any time of day.

"I thought you would. I guess we like the same things, don't we?"

"I guess."

"A lot of days, this is the only time I can come here 'cause I'm at work till five o'clock. But I think I'd choose this time as my favorite anyway. Do you feel the same?"

"Yeah, I guess."

"I thought you would. You and me have a lot in common, you know that?"

This time you just nodded.

"You know what else I like to do, which you can only do when there's no one around?"

"What?"

"I like to take my suit off for a few seconds and just feel the air. The air feels good on you, and it feels good to swim with nothing on, too."

Ray was already sliding his trunks off.

"But isn't it against the law?"

"There's no rule in the grove about it. And no one can ever know about it 'cause they aren't out here with us."

You shrugged again, aware that it was too ambiguous and weak a gesture. Joey had once threatened to pants you and had once halfway succeeded with Peter and another kid before they jumped in on their own into the lake (you all called it committing suicide). But this was different.

"There's nothing wrong with it," Ray added. He was sitting next to you with his tight blue bathing suit around knee level and you couldn't help staring at his enormous penis, more like a horse's penis than a man's. Meanwhile, he moved his legs slightly apart as if to improve your view of it.

Ray asked you again, and this time you said you were tired, which immediately struck you as a lame thing to say. It occurred to you that at the Stockbridge Beach there'd be a lifeguard (just out of shouting distance now though visible like some kind of emperor in his high, white chair suspended in the sky). If you'd only gone there to swim this wouldn't have happened.

"How can you be tired at your age?" Ray said, his teeth visible, as if they too had an erection.

Again you shrugged, but you were already starting to tremble.

"How old are you?" Ray said.

"Fifteen," you answered, suddenly trying to sound older. In any case, it didn't work.

"You're old enough to swim any way you want to. Come on, we can dive in together and you can take off your suit in the water behind the raft. No one will see us, I promise." He put his arm around you. His long-fingered hand rested on your shoulder. His penis looked like some giant ornament on a Christmas tree.

Then you stood up. "I've gotta get going," you said. And a second later you jumped into the water and began swimming toward shore. You remember thinking you shouldn't swim as fast as you could because that might alarm Uncle Ray, and you worried that he might swim after you. He was an excellent swimmer, perhaps the fastest in Beachwood, and could catch you in a matter of seconds. You could picture him moving toward you like a shark.

When you got to the beach, you picked up your towel from the sand in one motion like you were fielding a ground ball. You felt an overwhelming temptation to turn around and look at Ray (was he swimming behind the raft? was he still on the raft, maybe standing and waving at you or perhaps just staring at you? or was he swimming after you as you feared?), but you resisted turning to look. You walked quickly but not too quickly through the grove. You looked at the pine needles, then at the wooden sign nailed to an evergreen tree that said, "No dogs, bikes, or ball playing," three rules which the community broke virtually every day.

Then you picked up the pace a little, and because you were in a hurry, you stepped on a stone that hurt your foot and later stubbed your toe on a tree root. When you reached your favorite birch tree, you looked back and thought you saw him on the raft. Then you walked out of the grove and, when you were sure he couldn't see you, began to run on the winding mud path—thick green ferns on either side of you—because you were late for dinner.

You were only mildly rebuked by your father in his own quiet way. It was as if he had turned down the volume on everything he ever felt or said at home those days. Your mother echoed him, as you expected. They were like two lines of unintended poetry that couldn't help rhyming. Meanwhile, your brother took advantage of the situation to make fun of you in still another way.

"What's the matter; did you get lost?" he said.

You remember feeling relieved at first that you weren't going to get in trouble. That your father wouldn't yell at you (although he rarely did, it always seemed as if he could). Besides, the look in his fierce and disappointed eyes, though he never looked directly at you, made it seem as if he was yelling, which was just as awful in its own way. Was the world a choice between your family's cold avoidance and what you had just experienced with Uncle Ray?

Something terrible was happening to your parents, you realized that night, in its own quiet, immutable way. They were acting more like mechanical dolls than people, as if they had been robbed of whatever spontaneous parts of their personalities that still existed. They weren't openly hostile to each other but they generally spoke as few words as possible, and they acted as if eye contact could lead to a fatal disease. Meanwhile, your brother was rebelling in his own indirect way, never doing anything he could be punished for while mastering a sarcastic way of speaking that made his feelings about things that he'd never say directly unmistakably clear.

Your parents went to a movie that night in Pittsfield, the better to avoid the bitter requirements of conversation, you supposed. You made a half-hearted attempt to ask your brother if he wanted to play catch or just "do something" but he said no to both. Within a half hour, he had driven the car your father gave him for his high school graduation into Stockbridge, where he went to drink and meet girls.

Alone in your rented cottage, you realized that your brother, who was soon headed for college and New York, would never spend a summer at Beachwood again. Even if he did, he was already lost to you as if he'd somehow drowned in the lake.

But you also began to suspect that your parents wouldn't come back either, as you, yourself, wouldn't for many years. In less than a year, they were divorced. You'd worried that night that you might weaken and tell them about Uncle Ray, but you didn't tell them ever. You never told the whole story to anyone else either, though you dreamed about it quite a bit and thought about it when you least wanted to for a few years. A couple of times when you were drinking (once with a guy, another time on a date with a girl) you told a short version of it but in a comic way filled with alcohol-fueled laughter as if it were all a joke. And then you never spoke of it and learned to rarely think about it or even see it in your mind's eye, as if it were a fish you trained to stay underwater.

You notice that the man who might be Uncle Ray is putting

on his unappealingly green T-shirt. You watch him for a few seconds and then dive off the raft, swimming toward the shore, determined to find out who he is. When you reach the shore, his back is to you as he picks up the newspaper he was reading and a white towel, which he apparently never used. Your eyes are on him every second as he starts walking into the grove. You continue to walk ten paces or so behind him, deciding that you'll follow him home if you need to. After all these years, you think, he must acknowledge what he'd done. Also, he must apologize for giving you a memory so detestable that you apparently trained your mind to bury it (although you've re-experienced it your first day back, as if all this time it was waiting to ambush you).

He's walking over the thick pine needles, past the birch tree by the evergreens, where you, perhaps, once played catch with him, heading toward the fern-lined mud path that leads to the road. Finally, perhaps because he hears your footsteps, he turns his head and you see his face. At first, it's like looking at the sun too closely. You can't really see anything—the price for looking too closely. Then his face finally comes into view. You know you have to account for the way time has changed it, but you still can't tell if it's Ray. He is balding, but Ray could well be balding after all this time. The same as far as the glasses the man is wearing and all the weight he's gained, especially in his face and neck, but really all over. There is only one way to tell for sure: you have to see his teeth.

"Hi," you say.

The man turns his neck a little, then says, "Hey."

You can't see any teeth. But you want to force him to say a few more words so you can make a definite decision.

"Did you go swimming?" you say, as if it genuinely interests you.

"No, it was a little too cold for me."

You try to find something in the way he speaks that could identify his voice as being Ray's but can't. Voices are even harder to remember than faces after so much time has passed.

You are now halfway down the fern-lined path that leads directly to the dirt road. If you turn around now it will look more than suspicious, like you were trying to hit on him but got discouraged when he didn't stop walking to talk to you. Now, you know you will have to follow him out to the dirt road, although you'll eventually have to walk back to the grove to get your shirt and towel.

"Do you own a place here or...?"

"I own a home in Beachwood," he says.

You hope he'll stop walking then and turn around to talk to you so you can try to see his teeth again, but for whatever reason, he is in a hurry and doesn't turn around. Suspicious behavior, perhaps, but hardly decisive behavior. In your mind you hear your brother mocking your "lame" conversation. Then it occurs to you that if the man *is* Ray, he might not remember you, for you, too, have been changed by time.

As the road approaches, he stops for a second to be sure there are no cars coming and then crosses, heading toward his blue sedan. You, too, have to keep walking to get to the road as if you are also on your way home. Then, just after he closes the door to his car, you say, "Excuse me, are you Ray?"

He looks irritated for a moment and then waves. Maybe he waves because he doesn't hear you or maybe he does, or perhaps he just thinks you'd said goodbye and so to not be rude, he waves at you. Then he is gone—the new ghost in your life.

You return to the grove, past the thick ferns, over the winding path, then back to the grove toward the lake, still as a dreamscape, where your clothes are waiting for you on one of the deserted white wooden chairs.

You look briefly at the hills across the lake. They look like big purple splotches in the sky though there is still an orange sunstreak just above them, lighting the hilltops and part of the sky.

You turn your back to them and start walking. You could leave the grove on a different path that is wider and brighter but leave instead on the fern-lined mud path as if by going on the same route you might eventually see the man again who might be Uncle Ray.

But do you really think he's Ray, you ask yourself, just as a mosquito bites your leg. You review everything you remember from your short and banal conversation and have to admit that he almost certainly isn't. You wish him to be, perhaps, for some reason but he isn't. You go from fury to emptiness. You are furious at the real Ray but not at his stranger stand-in. The real Ray is still alive in your mind all these years later, apparently, as if by an act of magic. And the final trick is that he'd made you forget him while you were deciding where to go on your vacation, made you think the Berkshires were bad-memory proof. (That is when you start thinking about finding his boat, assuming he still has it and you can remember what it looked like, and taking it out to the island, then letting it loose or else just setting it on fire. But that doesn't happen.)

When you get to the road, the sun has gone, just dropped out of the sky. There is no trace of the man or his car. You stand off the road a little and pee into a clump of ferns. Then, carrying your clothes and keys, you head down the road away from your car. The phantom Ray, as you now think of him, might be looking for other boys out walking, boys who might also be late for dinner. Of course, that is a somewhat irrational thought.

You had forgotten how maze-like this walk would become—how many little dark roads would intersect the main dirt road, how many forks there'd be, how easy and dangerous it would be to get lost. Back when he used to socialize, your father was once dropped off after a bridge game twenty feet from his cottage and got lost anyway. Didn't get back home for almost an hour. The trees were so tall and thick they blocked out the stars.

You keep walking a little more and then realize you have already forgotten what the phantom Ray looked like. He, too, is now fully a ghost, and soon will be a faceless ghost unless your mind will give him an imaginary face, assuming it still can.

You come to another fork in the road and turn left, vaguely aware how quickly the dark has come. You walk less than a minute and then hear another set of steps in front of you. Instinctively, you double your speed, until you see it is a boy half-running home, probably late for dinner as you were the day you saw Uncle Ray. You wonder if Ray had followed you—probably not that evening—but other times. You also wonder if he'd watched you through your window when you were changing. If, thin as he was, he'd hid behind a birch or evergreen tree, waiting for you to undress.

You think of running after the boy to be sure he isn't lost or in any kind of trouble but are worried you'll scare him and so slow down. You've soon lost sight of him then lost the sound of his retreating steps as well.

You, yourself, are now lost as a result of following the boy, and yet the space around you looks strangely familiar, as if you were revisiting a dream. For some reason, in spite of yourself, you look briefly for phantom Ray's blue sedan, but realize you probably can't distinguish its color now from the surrounding black into which it has disappeared. Then you stop thinking about him but continue to walk into the area the boy had led you to. There is something about the shape and size of the trees and the cottages they hover over that is oddly familiar. Something familiar about the little creek that trickles to your right. You turn as if led by the water and follow it as you had followed the boy. Then you stop at the third cottage on your left. It looks gray, like it is drained of color, but you recognize it even in the dark as the cottage your family rented that last summer in Beachwood. You can't tell if anyone is home who could help you back to the road where your rented car is parked, but you sit down on the wooden steps that lead to the porch anyway. If the family that lives there sees you, you'll explain. If they don't, you are prepared to stay the night sitting there. You could finally put on the clothes you've been carrying from the beach which would make you warm enough, you suppose.

You stare at the small, slightly lopsided cottage where you'd spent so many summers with your family until in your mind's eye you can finally see each one of them with their characteristic expression of that last summer—a kind of quiet terror just perceivable behind an immobile frown. You think you'll leave then, but you keep sitting there and staring until you finally see each one of them at an earlier time when they smiled enough that you could see parts of their teeth like tiny stars in the night.

You come back to the present and stare again at the house— the last place you had all tried to live together. Finding it as you have at the day's end, you don't know whether to shed a tear or laugh. You ended up doing both.

The Chill

A MAN walks into a bar and decides that he will tell a joke beginning with those exact words—"A man walks into a bar." He feels that he's really been a kind of crypto-comedian all his life and wants a chance to show it, if only to the people seated at the bar. Just before he opens the door, he realizes that he'll let in too much cold air. He shuts the door before he even tells a single joke. Instead he takes a walk up Chestnut Street and thinks about his childhood as if the wind blew it forcefully into his mind. He remembers pulling his blanket up over his ears when it was cold and how he felt like he was in a tomb of ice.

One night when he couldn't sleep because he felt so cold, he called for his father and told him his problem. His father opened his closet door and put three more blankets over him. When that still didn't work, his father started telling him silly jokes one after another, like "Do you know why the basketball died? Because it was shot so many times." He laughed after every joke his father told, and kept asking for more. Just before his eyes closed, he saw his father tiptoeing out of the room. It was perhaps his favorite memory.

. . . . .

"The wind lives in a seashell," his mother told him at Revere Beach. "Put the shell over your ear and you can hear it talking."

He did what his mother said and heard the wind.

"Does the wind have a family or does it live alone?"

She looked at him as if he'd asked the wrong question. He knew then that she didn't know. That no one did.

. . . . .

His parents had let him go to the movies by himself in Boston. His house was only ten minutes away by streetcar but still he had the feeling of having taken a substantial journey, and because he was by himself, he felt both excited and a little nervous. It was late fall, and the wind blew leaves around Boston Common. He knew he should take the subway home now but instead looked around at the vast green lawns of the park while dodging the leaves that occasionally flew toward him like little birds. Suddenly, he saw two teenage boys fighting a third who appeared to have a dog leash tied around his neck. Then a new figure approached him, older and larger with wild green eyes but vague features, as if his face were made of watercolors.

"Wanna take a walk with me?" the man said, holding a different leash.

He started running down Beacon Street as fast as he could without once looking back. Good thing he didn't pick the park to run through as it was mysteriously empty except for the fighting boys and the man who was half-yelling, half-laughing at them.

. . . . .

The wind has its own sound but it's also part of every other sound. The dinosaurs heard it—they just didn't write poems about it, he thought. He remembered the way the sink faucets moaned in his parents' cellar. It was a muted but oddly terrifying sound, like a devil choking. But one afternoon, when he was alone in the cellar, he heard it in a different way and didn't run upstairs. Instead, he kept pulling himself wildly knowing that this time he wouldn't stop until he exploded. He could feel it piercing forward like a hot wind building inside him. Then it spilled out onto the cellar floor. He stood over it, astonished, as if it were both dead and alive.

. . . . .

A man walks into a college talent show. He is a student living away from home who thinks he has a gift for making people connect through humor. He tells some mild sex jokes, some observational humor à la Jerry Seinfeld, but steers clear of politics and religion. Things are going pretty well until he starts to shiver. He becomes afraid that the audience will notice it and be distracted from his monologue. He begins to think more about his shivering than his jokes and starts to lose the audience. Later some of his friends tell him he was funny, but he knows they're lying. It is the last show he ever performs in public.

. . . . .

Shortly after college, after he moved to Philadelphia and began working at an insurance company, he felt the chill again. It was as if it had been following him since his childhood and had finally tracked him down. He was returning from a restaurant when he felt it pass through him like a small, violent wind. Since there was a kind of wind tunnel near his apartment where he was walking, he didn't think much of it, figuring it was something that would go away in a few seconds. But the cold persisted even after he walked into his lobby and paid his respects to the doorman. He self-consciously paced around to lessen the chill that seemed to have targeted him, especially his neck.

It didn't get better in the elevator; in fact, if anything, it got worse. Fortunately, there were no other passengers, so he could press himself against the wall to try to create a feeling of warmth. Shortly, though, he realized that was only an illusion.

He wondered if anyone else felt it. The doorman didn't look any different bent over his racing forms, but how often did he really look at the doorman in a careful way? So he couldn't really evaluate the doorman's behavior.

What about the people on the streets? Any unusual activity there? Again, he hadn't noticed, but ever since he moved to Philadelphia by himself he'd followed his parents' advice to look straight ahead and never make eye contact with a stranger, though, of course, almost everyone was a stranger.

He began using a lot of blankets at night and wearing a heavy shirt over his sweatpants, but it made little difference. It was as if, ghostlike, the wind had invaded a part of him just above the base of his neck, where it couldn't be dislodged.

Soon he started seeing doctors. When he let each doctor touch his chill spot, or, more accurately, the chill's ostensible port of entry (since he felt the coldness internally as opposed to on the surface of his skin), they told him they couldn't detect any difference in temperature between his neck and any other part of him. He soon decided the doctors were as useless as rocks in the desert.

Then his dreams began, first about the doctors, then about the chill itself. In one dream he was running from the chill, looking over his shoulder at it as he ran towards his apartment. The last time he looked, he saw a face forming on it but he couldn't recognize it. It didn't really look like a human face and yet it was nonetheless strangely familiar. If he had a close friend in the building or even in the city or if his parents were in Philadelphia, of course, he would have screamed their name. He thought of the phrase "Life is a scream" as if it were skywriting made by an invisible plane. He pictured his doorman bent over his racing form. Everyone was always monitoring their luck. They had their luck, and he had his chill. He was running so hard now that he felt he was burning—burning and freezing simultaneously.

When he woke up and focused his eyes he was completely dressed, sitting on his couch, no longer sure if he had really been chased by the chill or if he'd dreamed it. He was breathing heavily, panting like an animal, slowly trying to retrieve his breath.

He called his friend Fennel on the phone who told him perhaps he needed to get online and meet a woman. Obvious advice, of course, but coming from Fennel, his best and only friend, it had impact—enough for him to join dating sites and to devote some free time each day to looking at profiles and sending out his own.

There was a woman named Vicky whose kind of cheerful aggression appealed to him—frankly, since he'd left home for Philadelphia, he'd lost some of his own. Also, her emails were kind of funny; perhaps she would discover his "inner comedian," as he now thought of it.

She suggested a place in Rittenhouse Square he hadn't heard of, but then, although he ate out at least one meal every day, he hadn't been keeping track of any restaurant names. The place turned out to be lively and not too pricey—an excellent and considerate choice on her part.

She wore black designer jeans with a classy pink top. He could see she had a good body. She smiled and laughed a lot, but not too much. She seemed to have a lot of experience with quiet men like him. She worked as a legal secretary but wanted to write children's and young adult books—maybe one day start a small publishing company of some kind. After a glass of wine, he admitted that he wanted to be a comedian and hadn't completely given up the dream yet.

She thought this was "marvelous," clapped her hands, and literally squealed with delight. Not since his mother had a woman reacted with such enthusiasm to something he said.

"You're amazing!" she exclaimed.

Instinctively, he turned away. He didn't want her to see that he felt he was in love with her already.

"You're probably wondering why I haven't said anything funny so far."

"First of all you have—in a low key kind of way, and I like low key. And second, I know you comedians are often serious people who make comedy out of your pain."

That seemed to open the door even wider and they began to confide more things in each other—especially her. She told him she was just starting to date again after a long relationship.

"That's rough," he said knowingly, although his longest relationship was scarcely a month. After two more glasses of wine he invited her to dinner.

"I've got an idea. My place is only a couple of blocks from here. Why don't you let me fix you some food," she said.

"No, I couldn't let you do that."

"But I'd love to. I have some Chinese and some really nice French hors d'oeuvres. Believe me, they're too scrumptious— it'll wreck my diet if you don't help me eat them."

He looked genuinely incredulous. "I can't imagine you needing to be on any kind of diet."

"Watch out, James, you seem to know how to really get to my heart."

He laughed—he hoped not too loudly. When she said "heart," he wanted to think of her soul; instead he pictured her chest that covered it. Yet apparently he'd escaped detection (after all, he shouldn't think of her as a mind reader), and she still seemed eager to take him to her place.

Her apartment was orderly and feminine, and the colors of the living room matched well. It was lit just brightly enough to be romantic, he thought.

She motioned to a sofa and they sat down together. They spoke for a few minutes and then she suddenly kissed him and said, "Food can wait a little while, can't it?"

He felt she was borderline drunk and that it wasn't fair but who was he to resist her. He pictured Fennel, the closest thing he had to a sibling, telling him he was a fool to resist her.

They kissed relentlessly for a minute or two. Soon clothes started to fly off like leaves in the wind. She told him to sit on her carpet, then she slid up to him, put a hand on his head, and pointed him down to her genitals. Meanwhile, she was moaning in an oddly musical way. The singer and the comedian, he remembered thinking, as if they were a stage act.

He felt she had an orgasm in his mouth, though he couldn't be certain and was afraid to break the spell by asking. Meanwhile, he was getting erect and a little sore in his knees so he got up to enter her.

"Stop! What are you doing?" she half-screamed at him.

"Oh, don't worry, I have a condom."

"Worry? I'm not worried, I'm not doing it is what's happening."

"But I thought—"

"Don't think. Just listen. I'm not ready for that."

"Oh."

"Yeah, 'Oh,' " she said, clearly mocking him. "I'm going to give you the benefit of the doubt, otherwise you could be charged with raping me."

She was staring at him. There was an odd tattoo by her vagina but he couldn't read it without staring at it and he certainly wasn't going to do that. He forced himself to look at her eyes. She seemed a little calmer now.

"I'm sorry there was a misunderstanding," he said.

"Yeah, so am I. You better get your things on now and leave."

• • • • •

For a long time he thought about his ill-fated date with Vicky. Finally, it hurt a little less every day to remember, as Fennel had predicted. But then the chill returned, albeit briefly, not in his dreams but in his waking life.

There is always a way to reassure ourselves, he thought, hence the saying "Where there's life there's hope." In his case, he thought that the chill happened much less frequently in his apartment, yet of course when he thought some more about it, he had to concede that might not really be the case, that even if it did happen less frequently in his apartment, when it happened it was often unbearably intense—so that the next time he felt it, he went out in the night as if he had no choice. He thought that if the chill were in his home then he was essentially homeless. Your home is the death of choices, he thought.

He walked a block and a half into Center City with no sign of the chill. He even undid the top button of his winter coat (which he wore although it was already early spring). He was struck by how bright and festive the city looked. Every place was intriguing and strangely filled with charm. He tried to stay calm and rein in his tendency to romanticize things. Things weren't more beautiful than before, he told himself. He was simply able to appreciate them more because the chill wasn't chasing him.

Another block passed. People seemed to be smiling at him—what was he to make of that? He decided, superstitiously perhaps, to stay on his same route at the same speed heading downtown through Center City. He would not undo another button, though he was tempted to, and would continue to look at his city with both admiration and trust.

But then, like the first signs of a toothache, he started to feel the chill again, and before he could walk another block it was already gnawing at him.

He broke into a trot then, soon deviating from Center City. A moment later he turned left onto a side street and ducked into a bar breathlessly, where he sat next to a thin blond man in a black T-shirt and black cowboy hat.

A man walks into a bar quasi-hysterical, he thought, and doesn't know whether it's worse to talk about what happened or keep it to himself.

"Hey, pardner," the cowboy said, turning slightly towards him and in the process almost making eye contact. "You OK?"

"Sure. Why do you ask?"

"You look like you just seen a ghost. Other than that, no reason."

The cowboy was smiling although he couldn't tell the color of his eyes, only that they were part of a smile in progress. He forced himself to laugh strictly to be polite to the cowboy before realizing that now he'd have to say something at least remotely true about his general condition.

"Well, I guess you're right."

"Yeah, I thought so. Are you shivering because it's cold or 'cause it isn't?"

"It just hasn't been the best night of my life."

"Sometimes you gotta fish for a long time before you feel any kind of tug on your line."

He looked hard at the cowboy in the half dark of the bar and thought maybe he really was a cowboy. The way the light in the bar was, the cowboy's head seemed still and strangely suspended, like the work of a taxidermist.

"This your first time here?"

He felt his heart beat as if the chill were already hovering nearby in the bar.

"Why? You come here often?"

"Yeah. That's why I asked you if you've ever been here before. I figured I would have noticed you one time or another if you had."

Was there something extraordinary about this place, he wondered. He noticed then that it was entirely populated by men, some of whom were being overtly affectionate. Oh that, he thought. He'd have to make it clear to the cowboy where he stood on the issue.

"Sure. That makes sense," he mumbled.

"Care to dance?"

He wasn't even aware that there was music.

"No thanks, I'm a little tired."

He didn't feel like getting into the fact that he was straight. He saw a quick image of the boys in the park and their wild-eyed master.

"Sure, I get it, I'm a little tired too. Truth is, I'm exhausted."

"Why's that? Hard day at work?"

"Wasn't work so much as what happened after work."

"Oh. Feel like telling?"

"I did some running. Serious running," the cowboy said, looking at him incriminatingly.

"I admire you guys who stay in shape like that. Yeah, I really admire you runners."

The cowboy held up his hand in protest. "I didn't say I was a runner. Never said that."

"Oh?"

"Just that I was running today."

"Where to?" he asked, immediately thinking he was being uncharacteristically nosy. Maybe escaping the chill had affected his behavior.

"I was running after someone, tell you the truth."

Of course he wanted to know why but he held his tongue. For several seconds they sat in silence.

"Bet you want to know, don't you?"

"I wouldn't be human if I didn't, would I?"

"I don't know. There are so many different opinions about what makes someone human these days."

"I hope in any group discussion on the matter I'd get voted in?"

"To what?"

"Humanity."

"Oh. You never know about things like that. People are so …slippery."

He smiled, not sure if he should laugh or not.

"Anyway," the cowboy said (he noticed that his Western or pseudo-Western accent had temporarily disappeared), "I was actually running after you."

He stared at the cowboy intently and then turned his head away as if he'd just looked too directly at the sun.

"What do you mean?"

The cowboy smiled thinly while a series of peculiar expressions seemed to fight for supremacy on his face.

"Can't say it any more clearly. Hasn't anybody ever run after you before?"

His immediate temptation was to say no but then he thought about that man in the park back in Boston.

"But why would you do that?"

"Do what?"

"Run after me? Did you think I'd dropped my hat or something?"

"No."

"I mean, you don't even know me, so why would you run after me?"

"I didn't say I knew you just that I ran after you. Did the other people who ran after you all know you?"

A valid point, but one he didn't feel like pursuing. Maybe the cowboy was only acting out some fantasy, or making some kind of avant-garde pass at him. It would have been much easier to have just danced with him.

"I seem to be making you uncomfortable," the cowboy said.

He shrugged.

"I'm going to use the men's room for a minute, but don't worry, I'll be back, and we can talk some more about this."

"Sure," he said, as neutrally as possible.

He was afraid to look in the direction of the bathroom, afraid to see the cowboy moving or perhaps in some way to see only the wind. Maybe the cowboy thought he was someone he knew. If he saw either of his parents in Boston he'd run after them. Perhaps that's what happened to the cowboy.

But that line of thought balanced against the cowboy's behavior wasn't really reassuring. It was preposterous and simply an unrealistic conclusion to reach. Wasn't it more possible, since he'd already asked him to dance, that the cowboy was trying to intimidate him in some way that would impress him, that he simply wanted him sexually? He himself had lived long enough to know that people of all kinds were capable of acting that way, though he had never been that aggressive. His night with Vicki was proof of that. He was always the pursued and never the pursuer.

He got up from the bar then and walked to the door. Fortunately, he hadn't bought a drink yet so he wouldn't have to be delayed by paying for it.

For a block, he walked at full speed, then broke into a run. He didn't hear or feel anything but the sound of his running, the strange music his shoes made on the sidewalk. He remembered as a kid trying to outrun a dog that eventually bit him. He always thought he could have avoided the bite if he'd just run a little faster.

Colors streamed by him like water as he ran into the wind, his eyes tearing like little windblown ponds. He had no concept of direction. Soon, it was like running into a blizzard. For a long time he ran this blind blizzard run, then finally he saw his building tall and proudly monolithic like a fortress at the top of a hill.

The doorman gave him a funny look as he walked by but what did it matter? People could only really judge you if you let them.

When the elevator came he was ready for it. A woman from his floor who rarely talked to him felt an impulse to quasi-acknowledge him with a nod which he happily returned. It was strangely reassuring. There was no ensuing conversation but that was OK, perhaps better to protect the moment which words so often destroyed.

A muted chill crept somewhere between his neck and left shoulder but it wasn't freezing. Now it felt more like a cool spot in a warm desert.

When he got inside he went directly to his room. On the bureau were two 5" by 7" silver framed pictures of his parents. In one his father was wearing shorts that showed his hairy legs. He was smiling at him. His father had even taken his glasses off for the photograph. In the other picture, his parents were kissing while he sat in front of them, no more than three years old, playing in the grass. He thought of calling them but they were probably already in bed. Instead, he sat on the edge of his bed and stared at his parents. It was odd to stare at them but it was also calming. A moment later he realized the chill was gone, and then, with all his clothes on, he lay down for a minute and fell asleep. When he woke up he felt he was in a warm green park shaped like the yard of his childhood, a shining blue sky overhead. Peace is temporary, he thought, but always blessed.

The Offering

THE FIRST time was when his mother was crying. He reached in his pocket, opened his hand, and offered her a nickel in the hopes that she'd make up with him. He didn't remember her exact reaction—he was only about five—but her tears stopped as if a waterfall suddenly ceased falling. The sky too, gray and listless, suddenly brightened. It was like nature itself instantly changed because of his nickel. Of course he tried it again the next time she started crying or else repeating the same stories with the same words, and it seemed to work again, at least a little. Later, when he got older, he sometimes gave her flowers thinking he'd do anything to hear her laugh and tell jokes again (she could be so funny and was an excellent mimic) or else simply hug him again, which she always seemed to want from him.

· · · · ·

He was in New York the first time he paid a woman for sex. He never used an escort service—always trusting the street instead. Her name was Sunshine—of course not her real name, he assumed. She was a pretty, young black woman, somewhere in her early twenties, dressed just flamboyantly enough to identify herself without overdoing it. She was working on the fringes of Hell's Kitchen near Times Square. Negotiating with her was easy, as was talking to her in general. She had an oddly appealing personality, too, not bitter or withdrawn like so many other hookers he'd meet later.

Everything worked well once they got to his small apartment on the upper West Side. His only regret was not setting up another date right then and there, though she assured him he'd see her again on her usual street. But he never did. Hookers are like fireflies, he thought. They appear and disappear just as they make your money do the same.

It was different with Courtney. He picked her up at a party in New York. For the first week or two he didn't know she was a prostitute. He remembered that she was from Canada and was very generous. She took him out to dinner and gave him free cocaine. He found out what she was doing because she kept getting calls late at night and because she started canceling dates with him at the last minute. On the one hand, it was flattering that she did him for free, but he felt deceived and jealous, of course, and so ended it. He remembered making her promise to see a therapist, but as far as he knew, she never did.

He stopped doing it for a while after Courtney and went back to "regular relationships" through dating ads in the newspapers, but a few months later went out on the street again.

The next one was different. He was never sure of her name so he called her "48th and 8th" in his mind after the place where they'd met very late at night. It was pretty much the same place where he'd met Sunshine. 48th and 8th was really high on something and couldn't carry on much of a conversation. She was his first white prostitute (not counting Courtney) and, looking back on it, probably his first crack whore, too. She was trim and had pretty, albeit druggy, blue eyes. She mumbled something about the Carter Hotel, the Ritz of the hooker hotels near Times Square, but she ended up doing him in a parking lot near the Carter. A few days later, he met up with her, again, as he'd hoped he would, and this time he snuck her into the hotel. He remembered how they laughed—it was like playing hide-and-seek.

After that time in the Carter, he started looking for her on her block. A week later he finally found her very late at night again, and she did him in the same parking lot—fortunately, it was a warm spring night. But the funny thing was she didn't remember him, he could tell. Then she disappeared, and he remembered missing her as if he'd prematurely lost a girlfriend.

"Hookers aren't built to last," a fellow john once said to him, and he wondered how many of the girls he'd been with had made it past forty. He'd seen them mostly in his twenties and early thirties, just before the AIDS era kicked in and changed the business. It was probably lucky that he'd never gotten too close to them if they were all going to disappear (hooker talk for "die"), he'd figured.

Only once did he really get emotionally involved. It was during his late thirties while he was living in South Philadelphia. He was walking back from his soul-killing job as a copy editor (really a glorified proofreader for a company newsletter), not ready to face his empty apartment, when he saw her. She seemed to be shining on the otherwise featureless gray street. It was like seeing a healthy young woman emerging from a bombed-out village. She was wearing obvious hooker clothes; her cheap silver-colored skirt was hiked up nearly to her crotch, but somehow she still looked stylish. Her purple shirt was almost preternaturally pretty.

He walked up to her without any of the inhibitions that usually dogged him his entire life, he thought, even with prostitutes, and which usually led to his drinking before he approached them.

"Hey, I'm Mason," he said with a lot of self-confidence, he thought. She was literally standing in the street by the traffic light.

"Oh, OK, I'm Nicole," she said, making eye contact for only a split second as if afraid she might miss a Cadillac or Mercedes that could suddenly stop at the lights.

"You're certainly the best thing I've seen today," he said.

"Thank you."

He looked at her more closely and thought that she looked like his first real girlfriend who, at the time, had been a teenager.

"You're really very beautiful."

"Thank you, officer," she said, finally leaving the street and moving onto the sidewalk.

"Officer? I'm not a cop. Is that what you think? Far from it."

"Oh, yeah?"

"Yeah. That's not fair. I tell you you're beautiful, and you tell me I look like a cop."

"Some cops are pretty cool looking."

"I'll try to take it as a compliment, then."

Her eyes were on the street again, and he started to worry that a car might stop for her any second.

"So, what do I have to do to date you?"

"But, officer, I hardly know you. What would make you think I'd date you?"

Meanwhile, the cars whizzed by like guided missiles. It was both dangerous and strangely charming, something he hadn't felt for a long time.

Finally, he convinced her to walk to his apartment in South

Philly. She continued to talk in a joking but surprisingly articulate way. Not only was she probably the prettiest prostitute he'd ever met (or certainly high up on the list), but she also used the best grammar. His only wish was that she'd at least glance at him from time to time while they walked. Instead, she looked straight ahead, soldier-like. It made him feel frustrated and sorry for her at the same time. He wanted to ask her the inevitable question—why she was on the streets—but didn't. He could sense already how prickly she was and how proud.

Despite her best efforts, her emotions were always close to the surface, as she could cry or laugh hysterically at any given second. They walked upstairs to his apartment, and she wiggled her bottom to make him laugh. She continued to clown and tell him dirty jokes in the bedroom before she did him. But a minute after it was over she was already wiping away new tears.

He dated her whenever he saw her from then on over the next few weeks. Gradually, in fragments, and possibly with some exaggeration, she told him about her life. She said that her father had sexually abused her and her mother was a heroin addict, so she couldn't turn to them for help. She said she was a nineteen-year-old racially mixed girl from New Orleans who went to college for a few months, but had to drop out to support her child. "Hope" (he assumed that wasn't the child's real name) was four now, and he came first. She had moved to Philly hoping to become an actress or model.

It was a brutal story, but she mixed in jokes from time to time, as if on cue, at just the right moments. When she was funny or light he didn't think he'd ever enjoyed listening to a person more. But when she got angry and repetitive or just sad, he felt depressed, too, and yearned to help her, especially after she showed him a picture of her son, who was now staying mostly with her hooker friends in Philly. That was when he started giving her extra money and buying her presents—once a dozen roses, though he realized later she had no place to put them. That was also when he offered to let her and Hope stay in his place for free. Since she was homeless, he thought she'd say yes, but she turned him down.

"I got a place to live already on my corner," she insisted. "I have a home with my name on it. Yep, I got a cardboard palace just for me."

She told him more about her life that day. It was a tangled tale he'd heard part of before, about her running from her father, then coming to New York, where she danced in strip clubs and fell for one of her bosses, who was also a dealer.

"Was he your pimp?" he asked jealously.

"I've never had a pimp," she said, but he felt she was lying—it was, after all, a standard hooker lie.

"I get black men and white men like you, too, because I'm mixed. I'm universal, Mason. And, believe me, Asian men like me, too."

He looked at her again and thought that much was true.

"Why would you think I need a pimp?"

"I don't. I just thought it was something that happened to girls."

"Things only *happen* to weak people, and I'm not weak…Hey, all this talk is making me hungry. You have any food?"

And so he fed her. Later, she talked more about Hope, who she said she saw every few days and who she swore she'd get back as soon as she got a job. "You know, maybe at a CVS behind a counter if I could get cleaned up a little."

"What's his real name, your son?"

"I told you, Hope is his real name. He's my son, so any name I give him is his real name."

"It's a beautiful name," he said quickly.

She said she was only fifteen when she had her son. She'd been in love with his father, but he was a meth head who had "disappeared" years ago. Then she abruptly changed the subject.

She could be sweet to Mason, but other times she could be nasty. Either way, she was inevitably late for their dates. He preferred remembering the sweet times instead of brooding over the bad as he'd done before in his "regular relationships." Once she gave him a T-shirt "because you're always complimenting mine." He didn't want to ask her how she got it. He hoped it was one of hers, and she hadn't spent her money on it, and also that she'd worn it at least once.

He told her he loved to travel and would take her anywhere she wanted to go, but they never went anywhere. They never went on a regular date, either. Once she called him at two a.m. (he was pretty sure she was on some kind of drug) and talked and cried for nearly two hours. He nearly talked her into coming over that time.

They only ate out twice, but every time she came over he gave her food and extra money. He used to buy her clothes, too, nice clothes that took a significant bite out of his paycheck, until she told him to stop because "When it comes to clothes, you haven't got a clue."

She routinely criticized how he dressed or his haircut, but it never bothered him. Instead, he'd laugh about it with her. His mother used to make the same criticisms, but he hadn't laughed then. He took that as a good sign about Nicole.

"Hey, Mason, why do you want to see me so much?" she said to him once. "Why are you always asking me out?"

She said this after they'd just had sex together. She was sitting on the edge of his bed completely naked, while he was covered by a sheet.

"Because I like being with you."

"Yeah, you must. You know what was cute? When you first saw me and didn't think I noticed you that day on the street, you took your glasses off real quick so you'd look younger." She laughed then, and he felt embarrassed. Then she said, "But I think you just like doing me a lot."

"That's true, but I like just being with you a lot, too."

She looked at him as if trying to figure something out.

"But don't you want a normal girlfriend, someone closer to your age, who you could see a lot more often, maybe even move in with?"

"That didn't work out so well in the past."

"Why not?"

He shrugged. "I always seemed to be trying to please them but never could."

"With girls you gotta lay down the law sometimes."

He laughed a little. "They don't usually like that a whole lot either. Maybe I didn't do it the right way."

"They liked being in control, huh?"

"Even then, they weren't satisfied."

"I guess civilian bitches are as crazy as us working girls."

"At least as crazy," he said, laughing.

A week later he offered her five hundred dollars to spend the whole night with him. It was a lot of money on his modest salary, but she told him "That's the minimum top of the line girls get for staying over. I'm actually giving you a break. Hey, don't you think I'm top of the line?"

"Of course," he said, and when he thought further about it, it didn't seem like that much money.

He spent much of the day cleaning his apartment and doing laundry. He also went grocery shopping so he'd have her favorite snacks on hand, and though he knew that such overtly romantic gestures were sometimes off-putting to her, he also bought her a pretty unostentatious bouquet of spring flowers. Finally, thinking they'd have a lot of sex that night, he invested in a new, deluxe brand of condoms.

As usual, Nicole arrived nearly forty-five minutes late, which made him nervous and angry. His mother couldn't stand it the few times when he was late, but it seemed that he was always destined to wait for women.

"Why are you so late?" he said, fighting down his anger when she finally appeared.

"Haven't you ever heard 'all good things come to those who wait'?" She was wearing a short, black skirt and his favorite purple shirt, as if she'd emerged from a dream.

"Wait for a while maybe, but that was too long."

"It should make you value me more when you finally do see me."

"I don't understand why you couldn't call me. I just bought you a new phone."

"Would you rather I just left now? Honestly, you're really bringing me down."

"No, of course not, I just wished you'd call me when you're going to be late. You can understand that, can't you?"

He looked at her. Her face was beautiful but pitiless.

"I had some things to do about my son," she said, taking off her clothes as she stepped into his room. "It's not easy to go out on an overnight date because of him. There are a lot of things I gotta work out. So, I'm hoping you'll show me your appreciation."

"Who's taking care of him?"

"Yeah, who? That's the question."

He got up from the bed, in part because he loved looking at her while she was so unselfconsciously naked.

"You could at least bring him over some time. I'd like to meet him."

"You?" she said, pointing at him as she got up from the bed and started pacing.

"Yeah, me. Is that so unbelievable?"

"You think I'm gonna do you in front of my son? I'd rather die than do that. Hope'll never see me naked."

"Of course not. I get that, but who says we always have to have sex every time you come over?"

He thought she'd like what he said, but again, he'd miscalculated. She turned and looked at him. Anger and something else he couldn't quite define were flashing in her eyes.

"You trying to get out of paying me, now that we're friends?"

"No, no, it's not like that."

"Damn straight, it's not."

"I'll give you money every time you come here. I always have."

"You don't *give* me anything. You pay me what I earn. I'm a businesswoman, don't forget that."

"Fine, I'll pay you whether we screw or not."

That seemed to calm her down, and she mumbled, "OK, Mason. Sorry I yelled at you. You know how I am."

After they had sex, they split a quaalude, and she became

much friendlier. He asked her about Hope, but she didn't want to talk. Instead she started asking him a lot of questions about his life.

He told her about his childhood and about his mother. "She should have met my dad," Nicole said. "They would have had a lot in common."

He forced himself to laugh in the hopes that she would, too.

"So did she ever do you?"

"My mother? No, not physically."

"Oh, you got off easy."

"I guess it's all relative," he said. "No pun intended."

"Hey, you got any more jelly beans?"

He liked that she ate gumdrops and jelly beans and other kid food. "Of course I do. They're in the drawer with the pot."

He watched her skinny arm open the drawer. She was thin with a pretty small chest and a pretty big bottom, just like his first girlfriend. And her brown eyes were like his old girlfriend's, too. At the time of his first girlfriend he was living away from home and figured he was finally done with his mother and her constant flirting and jealousy—done with both his parents for that matter. He thought he'd be involved in an exciting career and that he'd escape into a world of love as soon as he met the right girl. He found himself telling this to Nicole who asked him, in between jelly beans, "Why you give up on regular women so easily? You're still only in your thirties, right?"

"I never said I quit. It's just so much effort for so little reward. It was like a job, only I ended up paying my boss. But I never said I quit," he added.

"You said it's been seven years since you had a girlfriend, didn't you? Honey, you're a hooker hound, that's what it is. You're addicted to working girls."

"Just you," he said. He wanted to add, "I wish I knew if you like me, that it isn't just about business," but he didn't.

She smiled and shrugged, then ate some more jelly beans.

• • • • •

It was years later, more than he wanted to count, and he was back on Broad Street on the edge of South Philly, where he'd met Nicole. His father was dead now; his mother had slipped into dementia and no longer knew who he was.

He'd gone from business to business, mostly in sales, and now was back in Philadelphia to finalize a deal for the home company. He'd made out all right, though he was still single and often wished he wasn't. He'd gone to a bar to relax after his meeting when he started thinking about Nicole and ended up taking a cab to South Philly. In recent years, he'd begun to enjoy the feeling of being in places that hadn't changed that much over time, although such places were getting harder and harder to find. The block where he was now standing seemed to be just such a place. It made it easy to remember Nicole and to see clearly again the clothes she wore that first day, especially her purple T-shirt, which was a color purple he'd never seen before or since. How young he was then, with so much life in front of him. And Nicole was unspeakably young, almost a child. He wished he could have made her see how young she really was when he knew her and how much possibility she therefore had. People slip in and out of your life like ghosts, he thought. After she stayed overnight with him years ago, he only saw her once or twice again. Then, like a ghost, she vanished. He tried her number, but no one ever picked up and soon her phone (apparently like her) was out of service. He went looking for her a few times, asked a couple of other hookers if they knew where she was, but they claimed not to know her or just not to know. He had even thought of asking some of the johns that hung around the neighborhood but he couldn't remember any of their names. He could have searched harder, asked more girls, offered a reward, perhaps, but realized at best he only knew her first name.

Now, he was back on her corner on the gray street, half expecting her to shine in front of him again with her great brown eyes and purple shirt. Mixed, she said she was. He could remember it all, he thought, except he never found out her son's real name. Then he realized he'd never really asked beyond that first time, though she'd described Hope so tenderly he'd sometimes fantasized that he might become the boy's father.

He crossed the street, looking through a clump of skinny sycamores by the sidewalk and wondering if Nicole's son was still alive and, if so, what kind of man he had become. Mixed up, probably, but he was still a little mixed up, too. It was like the world made people get that way, like it was part of its cosmic plan. Anyway, the odds that both Nicole and her son were still alive seemed pretty small, though Nicole would only be in her late twenties or just turned thirty and Hope would be around fifteen. But hookers weren't built to last, a fellow john had once said to him—or was it Nicole herself who had said it?

He started walking towards his old place on Tasker Street where he had spent that one night with Nicole. He remembered how he had watched her sleep in the middle of the night, wanting her to wake up so he could make love with her again but also hoping she'd stay asleep so he could keep staring at her mysterious beauty.

Finally, his old apartment came into view. He began walking toward its steps where she had so often kept him waiting and where she'd once given him a lollipop as a peace offering. Another time she borrowed a jump rope from a little girl from the neighborhood and skipped rope in front of him, making him laugh uncontrollably.

Just as he approached the steps to sit down for a moment, a black woman in her fifties in a tattered pair of jean shorts, a torn, half-open T-shirt, and a fat smear of bright red lipstick approached him.

"You want something, mister?"

Her eyes weren't focused right, could barely stay open.

"No, I'm fine."

"I make you finer. Ten dollars," she said.

"Sorry, I don't think so."

"You don't think so? Ain't asked what you get for your ten dollars."

"What's that?"

"Whatever you want. Anythin' you want, mister."

Her eyes were drifting off again like little hovering birds, uncertain where to migrate.

She'll walk away now, he thought. Yet neither of them left. The woman walked a step closer and looked at his eyes. She had the kind of face that could be any age at all.

"I need ten dollars, mister. I need five dollars. I do anything."

He looked at her while he fished around in his pockets where he had a bunch of singles. He turned his back as he took them out and fiddled with the bills until he finally arranged them into a kind of tiny green bouquet.

"I tell you what. Here's ten," he said, handing them to her with a hopeful smile. "My gift to you."

"Thanks mister," she said, ambling off in her frayed sandals down the sidewalk, lurching a little from side to side. He watched her while she moved under the darkening sky, as if the sky was somehow swallowing her. Then he realized that he hadn't found out her name. He wished he had.

The House Visitor

IT'S HALLOWEEN, and I'm in a house again. Only a mother and her little girl live in it. I would have liked to have a better view of what costume the girl was wearing, but I couldn't get out of my cab to see—it would have been too risky. I think she was dressed as some kind of princess. The mother was holding her daughter's hand, and the girl was holding a paper bag where she'd deposit her candy. At first, I worried that someone else might be left inside their house to hand out candy to the trick-or-treaters, someone who I didn't know about, though I'd researched the house and have known for quite a while that only the two of them live there. But I was reassured when I saw a big bowl of candy (mostly M&M's and Skittles) on a straight-backed chair on their porch. Behind it on a piece of white cardboard was a sign handwritten in orange Magic Marker that said "Help Yourself." The sign also featured a picture of a witch on a broom that was probably hand-drawn by the little girl.

I've never been in this house before. When I worked briefly as an electrician, I'd see four or five houses before I visited them for real, and when I was a physical therapist years before that, I sometimes made house calls for the patients too weak to come to the facility where I worked. Now I drive a cab, and it's almost impossible to see anything inside the houses before I visit them. Much as I want to go inside as soon as I see one that appeals to me, I've learned to be patient. I've also found that when I'm finally inside, I'm richly rewarded—it's like stepping into heaven.

The house that I'm in now is a modest two-bedroom with a cellar and one bath. There's an upstairs, which I'll save till last (as I've said, I've learned to be patient). In the living room, the first room I see, there are a number of framed color photographs. One was taken of the gargoyles on top of Notre-Dame Cathedral; another is of the mother and daughter on a beach under a cloudless sky. Still another depicts the two of them on a city street, possibly New York. There is also one of them by the Arch and still another one of them in what looks like the Missouri Botanical Gardens here in St. Louis. So far there's nothing of the father, which leads me to believe there was a divorce in this family. This will be one of the things the house will eventually tell me.

When you visit a house, it's like entering a person's mind. (It's like entering their body, too, though in a more abstract way.) In the case of families, you're really entering their collective minds, as if you've gone inside a living museum. For example, in the house I'm in now, each of the knickknacks on the mantle above the fireplace tells a story. Some of them, like the seashells, are more obvious than others, though nonetheless powerful for that. Then there are others, like the stone giraffe I'm touching, that are more elusive. Perhaps it came from a gift shop at a zoo. I look at it more closely, and in some strange way it seems to come alive in my hand. It feels like I'm holding a rainbow. Then I put it back in its exact spot. I never take anything from my home visits. I never eat any food and rarely even use the bathroom. I don't want anyone to know that I visited their house. I have no wish to give them a scare like that so I go out of my way to be careful, especially about putting things back where they were.

It's not as if I haven't had a close call or two, however. My record isn't perfect. Once I was in a bedroom when I heard the front door open and a man and woman talking. I had to leave through the bedroom window and skinned both my knees when I landed on the ground. Then I heard the man yell at me as I ran through his backyard to the end of the block where my cab was waiting for me.

Another time, I broke a really nice ornament in a single lady's home by mistake. She had a turquoise-blue glass horse. I wanted to get a better look at it, and it seemed to explode in my hands. Now I don't pick up anything that can break.

I go into the family room next. Sometimes when I go into a room it's like walking into a dream where everything is alive but still, as if all the objects in it are underwater. That's what their family room is like. When I sit down in the blue reclining chair, it's like settling into the ocean, but then I quickly realized that's impossible. What I really feel is that I've settled into some kind of dream world that only *seems* like it is underwater. It's never as easy as it's supposed to be to separate dreams from the rest of your life, and I'm always suspicious of people who do. My father was like that. He had no use for dreaming (unless you count drinking as dreaming) and little use for me. In fact, he often turned on me, especially when he drank, and would give me quite a scare as he chased me around the house, bellowing my name. I was afraid of what he would do to me when he caught me. My only place of safety was on the top floor, which he was usually too tired to climb to. I'd hide in the attic closet then, where I only had the hornets to contend with. To this day, attics give me a scare, and I never go inside them when I house visit.

Well, once I did. It was in my first year of house visiting so I usually don't count it, but I did visit an attic in a two-story kind of starter home in Richmond Heights. There were no hornets there—mostly just a bunch of broken dolls, two deflated beach balls, and some quietly aging board games like Monopoly and Parcheesi. No hornets, but I felt stung anyway, and as I stared at the toys and games half buried in the boxes, I felt extremely sad.

It's odd to be awake in the present while thinking and actually seeing things from the past. When you think about it, there ought to be a time tense between the present and the past like a transition tense where life really occurs. But maybe I'm thinking this because I'm overly relaxed in the reclining chair. I haven't fallen asleep, of course—that would be the worst thing I could do. My number one fear, really, is to be asleep when the house owner returns.

· · · · ·

I get up from the chair with a start, uncertain where I am. Then I realize that, incredibly, I'd fallen asleep for a few minutes. I also realize that I'd forgotten to close the Venetian blinds. Somebody could spot me, as it's not completely dark yet.

I rush into the living room and look out the window for a sign of the mother and daughter, as if they might materialize any moment from out of the sky. Instead I see a kid (probably a girl) dressed as a witch next to a kid wearing a mask of the president. Then I back away from the large window near the front door, realizing that it's far more likely that someone could see me here than in the family room.

I don't spend much time in the bedrooms—there are only two of them, one slightly bigger than the other. I don't even examine the photographs on the mother's bureau, or the posters on her daughter's walls, things I especially love seeing. I am feeling a little dizzy, like I used to feel hiding in the attic from my father. Still upset that I'd fallen asleep in the blue recliner, I start pacing up and down the hallway. Then I remember that the last time I house visited I also fell asleep for a few minutes sitting on a couch, which wasn't even comfortable. Finally, I stop pacing and stand still in the hallway till my dizzy feeling subsides. I remember falling asleep in my attic a few times while my father blasted the house with his swearing. It was like playing a game of hide-and-seek with your life. Why was he so angry with me and my mother, too? It is a great mystery, but I won't solve it today—not when I am about to plan my exit. Anyway, it's almost impossible to know what's happened to us, much less why.

It's never easy to leave a house safely, and I've been caught or confronted one or two times. Once, when I was very naïve, I went to a different part of St. Louis. Not realizing it, of course, I walked into a crack house. After a couple of minutes, I saw that I wasn't alone. Fifty feet or so away from me a man of indeterminate age was talking to himself. I remember his shirt was torn and full of holes. A black woman approached me. "You using?" she asked.

"No," I said, finally realizing where I was.

"You want something from me? I'll do it."

"What?"

"Whatever."

It was something that I knew instinctively I shouldn't think about. I told her no again and ended up giving her five dollars. I never went to the inner city again, though when I think about it, the people in those crack houses are house visiting, too, like me.

One other time, near the beginning, I got caught by an elderly white woman who entered through a side door I wasn't aware of. I saw her, we saw each other, about thirty feet apart. She was holding a bag of groceries, which I was afraid she'd drop. Instead, after being frozen for a few seconds she walked into the kitchen and put the bag down on the counter. I worried that she'd come back with a gun.

"I'm from County Cab," I said (ironically, I started to drive for them less than a year later). I waited, frozen myself, worried that while she was in the kitchen she'd be calling 911. But a few seconds later she walked out to face me.

"I didn't call a cab."

I did a smart thing then. I repeated her address but with one digit off, which she caught and quickly corrected me.

"Oh, that explains it. Our dispatcher must have made a mistake. When you didn't answer the phone, I knocked on your door and when no one answered I took the liberty of letting myself in."

"But I was out shopping so I couldn't let you in."

"Of course, Ms. I understand now. There'll be no charge at all. I hope I didn't startle you. I apologize if I did."

She gave me a funny look, then looked at my face quite seriously, the way some people in museums study paintings, and said, "Can you let yourself out?"

"Of course," I said. "Again, I'm so sorry for the mistake."

· · · · ·

When there's a house in my dreams, it's always my father's, the one I grew up in. I myself have never been able to afford a house.

I've rented one once, though I had trouble sleeping in it, to such a degree that I couldn't even stay a whole year. Truth be told, when it comes to where I live, I'm an apartment kind of guy, which works out for the best, I think, as far as my safety goes, since there are no houses tempting me in my immediate neighborhood.

Last night, I dreamed of my childhood home in Kirkwood. My mother and I were talking in the kitchen. She was wearing her somewhat frayed-looking pink bathrobe, originally a Christmas gift from my father years before, which she wore with pathetic regularity every morning. It was probably the last nice gift he ever gave her. She was skinning a banana at the kitchen table while she talked to me.

Suddenly, we heard a sound like repetitive thunder. It was my father walking upstairs from the cellar, his favorite place to punish me. He walked into the kitchen and we looked at him, his face a maze of lines and scowls.

"What's going on here?" he said, staring hard at us.

Then I woke up, but for quite a while I couldn't tell if I'd dreamed that scene or merely remembered it. This used to happen to me a lot when I rented a house in Webster Groves and it was one of the main reasons I left before my lease was up. Not only did I dream more then but I also had some of my most vivid and awful memories, especially of my father chasing me while brandishing some weapon from the kitchen, often a knife or a candleholder, as I ran yelping around the house till I was finally able to make it to the attic.

One time when I was feeling hot and queasy and safe enough to slowly open the attic door, I heard them having sex (knowing my father as I did, I couldn't call it making love) in the master bedroom a floor below me with the door open. I remember wondering if she did it to allow me to escape from him. In fact, that was the way I began to remember it, and for a number of years it was one of my most cherished memories until I started to think it was really a dream too and not a memory at all.

Sometimes, it seems that dreams and memories both pursue me like separate clouds joined at certain indistinguishable places. It's hard to know which message is from your memory cloud, which from your dream cloud.

· · · · ·

Still standing in the hallway like a stationary cloud of nerves myself, I briefly try to reconstruct how I got here. It was the un-pulled blinds, which could reveal me to anyone in the street, especially to the mother and child, who must be used to looking at those windows whenever they return to their house. Finally, I enter the girl's room. I hear the front door open, followed by voices, talking and laughing like little unexpected bursts of wind. It is them, of course, and they are too near the front door for me to run by them. Quickly, I stand behind the girl's bedroom door, trying to make myself as thin as I can, as if I were a really long, skinny carrot. I try to make myself as quiet as a vegetable, too, while I listen to them talking.

"Mommy, look how many Twix I got!"

"Wow, lucky girl. You did get a lot of Twix. Let's put all your candy in the living room—or do you think it'd be better in the kitchen?"

"I think they'd be better in my room," the little girl says. Her mother laughs.

"No, maybe the candy would be better off in my room."

"No, in my room," the little girl says, laughing and squealing.

"How about the kitchen, as a compromise? But you promise not to eat too much, too soon? OK? You promise?"

I imagine the little girl promised. I don't hear it, but I imagine she either spoke softly or nodded her head. What would be next? Wouldn't the girl be going back in her room in a matter of minutes or, more probably, seconds? I move into her closet, which is packed with games and coloring books. What will I do if she opens the door to hang up her jacket? Girls aren't like boys; after all, they hang their clothes up. I am pretty sure I could run past her and her mother and get to the cab I am leasing. Maybe I could even get a fare or two, and in doing so, establish an alibi. But I hate to think of the hideous fright I'd give them, especially the little girl. It could haunt her dreams the rest of her life.

Their steps sound more distant now. First landing like drum beats, they gradually grow softer until they disappear. I imagine they are in the kitchen putting the candy into bowls. I realize I will have to stay in the closet until they both go to sleep.

Once, years ago, when I was in my early twenties, I believe, before I started house visiting, I actually lived in New York, which meant I lived in a world of apartments. I remember that I was buzzed into the apartment building of a woman I was dating named Annie. She told me to "make myself at home" while she finished dressing for our date. It was the first time I ever explored someone's home besides my parents'. I remember the odd excitement I felt when I opened her hall closet (about the size of the little girl's closet I'm in now) and ran my hands over Annie's coat and one of her silk scarves, then, kneeling down, touched her boots. She worked in a bookstore, as I recall, which fascinated me. Books were like rooms—you could visit a different one every day—so I imagined that working in a bookstore would be like living in a house with thousands of different rooms.

Probably I talked too much about her job over dinner. Once you express too much enthusiasm about something people start to get wary, though if you're clever enough in the way you express your enthusiasm, like Walt Whitman in his *Song of Myself*, you can become quite the heroic figure.

Maybe I should have gone to college and read more books, but my father didn't want me to, and who knew what my mother wanted. She was too scared of my father to ever disagree—not that it did her much good, though I guess things can always be worse. Simply put, my father either had no faith in me or else didn't want to spend the money.

"When you turn eighteen, you stop living off me and go to work. Don't talk to me about college," he said once, as if he were saying the word "cancer." "I found a way to work without college; now it's your turn, buddy boy."

I said nothing back to him and merely nodded, my usual approach when I had to respond to one of his impromptu commands.

When I lived in New York, I hadn't yet discovered the relief I could find from house visiting. If I had, I would have left the city immediately with its jungle of apartments, its muggers and their drugs. New York City, where the buildings loomed over you always like a herd of dinosaurs.

On that particular date in New York, we went back to Annie's apartment. I remember that at a certain point she went to freshen up, and I found myself sitting on a small, straight-backed chair in her room. I looked around myself, saw a family picture on her desk drawer of her parents and (probably) her sister on the beach. Everyone was smiling except the probable sister, who had a strangely intense expression, as if she thought she was about to participate in an event that would guarantee her immortality. I looked at Annie's poster on the wall of Jimi Hendrix, then at her black pillows on her pink bed, then at a little green plant on her desk, so discreetly placed I'd almost missed it. One might have found her room unremarkable, even ordinary, but not me. I look at people a little differently than most—as aliens. It makes them seem tremendously compelling. That was the first time I felt that way. Three months later, I left for St. Louis and began my house visits.

· · · · ·

Nothing like the sound of footsteps to snap one back to the present. I will myself to be as still as a corpse while the steps keep coming.

When I listen more closely, I am sure I hear two sets of steps. I have a strange thought then; I think I might already be dead in some way. Maybe my father had beaten me to death years ago or else shot me. He was bigger and stronger and faster than me under normal conditions, so how could I have escaped from him all those times?

The other steps are in the room now. I try to screw myself further into a carrot shape behind some of the clothes, knowing that if the little girl or her mother open the closet they'll turn the light on first. Then I put on my ski mask, which will disguise most of my face.

What would happen if they saw me? They'd scream, no doubt, or perhaps the mother would faint, or maybe they've already heard me and the mother is carrying a gun she'll use to blow me away.

I, myself, would probably scream, too, gun or not. I'd scream for my life, scream that I wasn't going to hurt them, or even take anything from them, scream as I did when my father cornered me because there were some times when he did catch me.

I can hear them talking again.

"You want to change into your PJs now?"

"I can do it myself, mom."

"OK, sweetheart. I'll run your bath."

"Do I have to?" the little girl said.

I don't hear what the mother says back, but the little girl's steps come back into the room. There's a minute of terror while she moves around that ends only when I hear her singing. I am not sure what song it is—some children's song—but her voice sounds preternaturally lovely. I think that would be something, if I could write a children's song that she could sing, one that would make her smile while she sang it. Could writing a song like that somehow redeem me?

Soon I see that I'll have to stay in the closet until they are both asleep, stay without moving or making a sound. In such a situation, the worst thing I could do would be to think of my father and the times I had to hide from him, but I can't help it. You would think he was the only person I had met in my life, I thought of him so much. You would also think I would instinctively protect myself by blocking him out of my mind as much as possible. Instead, I locked him in. It's true he was not always in a rage—I can even remember that he used to read to me much as the mother was now reading *Goldilocks* to her little girl. There were also the times we flew kites together in Forest Park and then, of course, the one family vacation we took in Atlantic City, the only time we all saw the ocean together. I remember him and my mother laughing together on the boardwalk. I remember playing catch with him on the sand.

My father was a man whose dreams were drained by time. That's why he had little use for dreamers. Nothing he dreamed of happening came true. He wanted a great love, a soul mate who would be an intellectual companion. My mother was a kind and simple soul (if any person can be said to be simple) but she wasn't the right companion for him. She was not only unambitious herself; she found his ambition, or ambition itself, incomprehensible. My father had dreams of building a big restaurant but couldn't pull off the financing. He worked for a travel agency but wanted to own one and then franchise it. But that never materialized either. He wanted a large family but had only me, and my lack of success in school tortured him.

The mother stops reading. I can hear the book close, and their voices lift in unison as if performing a ritual, which I suppose they are—the ritual of the goodnight kiss.

When the mother leaves her daughter, I start to feel extremely uncomfortable standing still for so long, always being careful not to make a sound. Also, I need to pee, but I certainly can't give into that impulse either. Civilization is basically the repression of impulses—you never really have a choice if you want to be part of it.

In the dark, I continue to think of my childhood. The one constant I come up with is that I always wanted to please my father and that when I was very young, I was able to, but never again. I don't know why I didn't try harder to please my mother. She was so scared of him and tried so constantly to placate him that she had only a flimsy identity of her own. I always see her, in my mind's eye, wearing the pathetically tattered pink bathrobe my father gave her—the present of a lifetime in her mind. I see her running around with plates and silverware, waiting on my sullen father. Then after he left her for his TV and alcohol, she'd work on a quilt or whatever in the kitchen, knowing that the living room was his territory. She was a sucker for sweet and/or patriotic sentiments. I remember the quilt she worked on that said: "Home is Where the Heart Is."

When I house visit, it's like becoming part of the owner's family in a way. Their house, however long I stay in it (my personal record is nearly seventeen hours), becomes my home, and yet has a kind of exotic quality to it as well. That's why when I have to leave it I feel a double horror, my fear of being caught on top of the loss of my latest home. This time I feel both feelings with equal intensity.

Then the strangest thing happens—I start to shiver. Although the house is warm and I have every reason to believe the girl is asleep, I start to shake as if I am standing in the middle of the South Pole. Worse still, I am afraid my shivering is making too much noise and will wake up the daughter who will then scream for her mother.

I can't wait any longer. I start to prepare myself to leave, mostly mental preparations. Then I grab hold of the door and slowly slide it open an inch at a time, thinking that doing it slowly will make me more quiet. It is surprisingly dark in her room. The closet is dark, too, but her room is darker somehow, though her clock functions as a kind of night-light. I ask God for only one thing: please don't make the girl see me. It would be awful for her mother to see me, too, but I'm ready for that, unless she is the type to shoot first and ask questions later. I have a short speech prepared for her assuring her I took nothing before I run out of her house. It would be best, of course, if I never have to deliver it.

Finally, I step out of the girl's closet, still quiet as a ghost, which gives me confidence that I can move throughout the house without waking anyone. I tiptoe to her opened door but stop just before I step into the hallway. I think that since I was so successful in being quiet I could close her closet door just so. When she wakes up, everything will look exactly as it had before she fell asleep. Of course, it is unlikely that she'll think anything of it if she sees her closet open when she wakes up, but there is also a chance her mother might see it and grow concerned, even figure things out. I don't want my homeowners to know I've visited their home. It's a kind of silent pact I have with them.

I start tiptoeing back to slide her closet door shut but my step is so light, it is like walking on velvet. I feel like I am, in my own way, doing a good deed, that the little girl might be disturbed if she wakes up to find the closet door open, that she might well think that a monster was in there at night and believe that the closed door protected her from it.

I calculate that I'll reach her sliding closet door in three more steps, though it is so dark, I'll have to repress my desire to speed things up. The first two steps go well but halfway through the third I inadvertently trip on the track that the door slides on and, incredibly, fall against the door and then into her closet, creating a terrible racket. The girl makes a sound as if she is up or is soon to be up. I scramble to my feet and run out of her room, leaving the mess behind me, trying to tell if the girl had said "Mommy" or not, but running, at any rate, as if she had.

Sometimes you can't perceive how loud a scream is, as if your ears will it to sound like a whisper. The girl did probably say "Mommy"; she probably screamed for her mother, who now is running towards me, flashlight in one hand, perhaps a gun in the other.

I barely look at her, only notice that she is wearing white pajamas. She lets out a scream herself.

"Jesus Christ! Don't hurt us, please. Just get out. I already called the police."

"Sorry," is all I can manage, there being no time to deliver my speech. I fumble with the door for a few seconds. Then I run into the black Halloween night. Right before the end of the street I turn left and run through someone's yard so the police won't see me, just in case they drive here that fast. For a while, I am sailing; then I nearly trip on a rock. I can't tell if some kid moved it there as part of a game or if it grew there on its own. A block and a half later I take off my ski mask and get in the cab. I turn its lights on and have just started to drive when I see two police cars passing by me, no doubt headed for the mother's house.

I say to myself "I'll never do it again" over and over as I drive down Dale and get onto Big Bend. The way our company works is the drivers lease their own cabs and pretty much determine their own hours. I had already arranged to have the night off so I could enjoy my house visit but I am so upset by the way it went—scaring the two of them as well as myself—that I call the dispatcher (who naturally makes fun of what he imagines was my failed date) to make myself available to drive. I need the distraction and the alibi.

I continue saying to myself, "Let me escape this one last time, and I'll never do it again." Words I used to say to myself when I was hiding in my attic, though I rarely ever knew what I had done wrong then, so how could I not do it again?

After I drive a mile or so down Big Bend and begin to relax a little, I realize that I probably am not going to get arrested and that neither the mother nor her daughter had seen my face. Then I start to look for fares. I realize that I probably won't keep my hysterical promises, especially since I feel so cheated by my last visit. Horrific as it was, I am also already missing the house.

I see again in my mind's eye the little girl in her white costume dressed as a princess. How proud her mother must be. And yet it's also true that when you create a life you also create a death, the one thing our futures all have in common.

It is with these puzzling thoughts that I continue driving into the night, looking for fares, already yearning for a new house to visit.

V.I.N.

THE EARTH throbs with evil, Rogers thought. It is stained with horror of a million kinds.

Lately, when he first closed his eyes to try to sleep, and sometimes right after he woke up, he'd see a massing of lizards in his room, like evil itself, crawling and jumping and hissing. It was a short vision but it was powerful and convincing. When it happened that afternoon after his nap, he dressed as fast as he could, put on a pair of sneakers, and ran out of his apartment. For a moment he wished he could talk to his father, who was dead, or maybe an earlier version of his mother, who now was chair-ridden, but inevitably, he decided to try Whitman, who was not only the smartest person he knew but probably his only friend.

Of course it was a terrible thing for Whitman, all those years he spent worrying about his father's death. Curse of the old father, Rogers thought as he crossed the street. He, too, had an old father, but he mustn't think of that, at least not until he reached the park, where he could sit on his favorite bench—the one facing the basketball court. He walked quickly, periodically checking for lizards, although he mostly knew they were a hallucination, until he was convinced there weren't any. Then at last he sat down on his bench.

Yet having an old father probably helped form Whitman's mind, Rogers thought, helped his insight into things. Helped him to be kind, too, despite his mysterious way of life and questionable business activities. Because how could Whitman be expected to function successfully in a conventional way? Still, Rogers had only known him for six weeks, and he knew he had to be careful because he'd put other people on a pedestal before only to eventually be disappointed.

Rogers looked at the court and saw two black kids playing one-on-one. Meanwhile, a third boy bounced a ball on the sidelines, waiting for his chance.

The last time Rogers saw him, Whitman was with a girl. She was nice enough, if a little on the surly side. Ultimately, though, without meaning to, she kept him from talking to Whitman the way he wanted to. He could only hope Whitman would be alone today, assuming he would be in the park as he had said he might earlier on the phone. It wasn't that Whitman was so nice to him, although he was nicer than most, but that he was onto something, he saw *into* things, Rogers was convinced.

He remembered again, as he often did, how they met in this park by this very bench. They were both watching a full-court game when Whitman began reminiscing about his basketball days.

"You still look like you could play," Rogers blurted. Whitman was tall, trim, and quite muscular.

"Thanks, man."

"With anyone," Rogers added.

Whitman smiled. "You look like you could play, too."

It was untrue. He judged himself at thirty-four to be at least ten years older than Whitman, but because of the way Whitman said it, for the moment he almost believed it was true.

From then on he figured out the times when Whitman went to the park, where he said he conducted a lot of his business. In fact, he often referred to the park as his "Office." (Rogers never asked him what his business was, and he tried not to imagine it.) At first his imprecise knowledge of Whitman's schedule tormented him and he sometimes waited in vain for hours. But that misery was all forgotten as soon as he saw him. It doesn't take much to make me discouraged, Rogers realized. Nor to make me hopeful, either.

What would he do now while he was waiting? He watched the kids playing one-on-one for a while then looked out at the mostly deserted park. It was not even three yet on a weekday so most of the kids were still in school. Rogers shivered. It was a cool March day but the ball players would still come out. A man had to shoot his jump shot, after all—that was a given.

A disheveled looking man on a bench ten feet away began talking to himself. There was a bottle next to him. Rogers looked at the bottle, at the grass and trees beyond the benches, checked once more for lizards, wondered if his unemployment check would arrive today, then looked briefly at the sky where some flour-white clouds were forming. One formation of clouds looked like two battleships about to converge. Rogers looked at it for a moment, then looked in front of himself and saw Whitman, or rather Whitman with a girl, as it turned out, the same girl he had seen him with before.

"Hey, bro. Rogers, this is Audrey. Audrey—Rogers," Whitman said.

"Hi," Rogers said, in as pleasant a voice as he could muster. Audrey forced a smile and he saw that her front teeth were chipped. She had short dark hair as black as a crow and looked vaguely Italian.

"Did you want to rap with me?" Whitman said.

"I thought maybe I'd see you."

"Cool, but I got to do some business, bro, but if you want to wait, I'll be back in fifteen or twenty."

Rogers didn't remember what he said. Probably he just nodded. For several moments he sat still. This had happened to him before. He figured he was the kind of person who was destined to be seen in fifteen or twenty minutes.

A loud sound suddenly disturbed him. The boys on the basketball court were arguing and had started yelling at each other. Rogers got up from his bench. He would not let this happen to him again. In his mind, he could still see the back of Whitman's long army jacket, the kind men used to wear in the 60s and early 70s. He would not wait for him like a legless lizard stuck to the bench. He began, instead, to follow Whitman and Audrey. At first he ran, as he hadn't since he stopped playing basketball. That was made easier because he soon saw that they were walking in a straight line. When they were only fifty feet or so in front of him he noticed that Whitman was holding hands with the girl, which surprised him since he'd thought (based on her appearance) that she might be some kind of junkie or prostitute. Perhaps the sight of her made him move too close as if to verify it, without first taking cover. Whatever the reason, Whitman turned and said, "Hey man, what's up?"

Rogers said nothing, was unable to take a step forward or backward. Meanwhile, Whitman started to walk toward him, leaving the girl behind.

"You OK, man?"

"Yeah, I'm OK."

Whitman looked at him closely. "Thing is, I was going to ask you if you wanted to come with us when I saw you a minute ago. Yeah, I'd been thinking about asking you before that, too."

"Ask me what?"

"If you wanted to come to a meeting today with me and Audrey."

"What kind of meeting?"

"It's a group of really cool people who share a common vision."

"What kind of vision?"

"One that could really help you, I think."

Rogers nodded. He knew he wanted to go right away and didn't know why he was playing hard to get.

"Does this group have a name?"

"Yeah, it's called V.I.N. Why don't you come along and join us. I don't think you'll regret it."

"V.I.N., that's French for wine isn't it?"

"Yeah, but drinking wine's not what it's about, although we do partake."

"So, why is it called V.I.N.? Are they initials that stand for something?"

Actually, he did know what it stood for—he'd seen signs about the organization's open house meeting in his Laundromat and on the bulletin board of the UPS store where he used to work—but he wanted to hear Whitman say it.

Meanwhile, Audrey, looking suspiciously at him, had come down to join them.

"They do stand for something," Whitman said. "They stand for 'Victims of Infinity and Nothingness,' but don't let the name scare you off. Come to the meeting and see for yourself."

"Yeah, it's way cool," Audrey said. "It'll change your life."

· · · · ·

There were about a dozen people at the meeting on the ground floor of the modestly furnished town house, many of them odd looking or oddly dressed. Each of them "testified," some for a few minutes, others a bit longer. At first, Rogers was puzzled by the procession of testimonies. When he tried to find a common thread that would connect them, all he could come up with was the repeated use of the words "infinity" and "eternal," which was what the world was, and "nothingness," which was what man was. If you didn't realize this, you were guilty of "small thinking." If you did realize this, you had to act accordingly. But how? Then he began to worry that he, too, would soon be expected to speak.

"I can't talk," he said to Whitman. "I don't have any idea what I'm supposed to say."

"Don't worry. You don't have to talk if you don't want to. No one expects a first timer to speak if they don't want to."

Then it was Whitman's turn to testify, and for the first time, Rogers listened closely. He used the same terms and made basically the same argument, although he did speak more emphatically about "the death of establishment morality" and the birth of infinity-based behavior. But what impressed Rogers was how forcefully and passionately he spoke.

"Is he the leader?" Rogers said to Audrey.

"He's second-in-command but he'll be the leader soon."

When Whitman finished speaking there was lots of applause and everyone seemed excited. Whitman gave Audrey a quick but big hug, grabbing a substantial part of her bottom. Rogers tried to concentrate on how he would congratulate Whitman but couldn't stop staring at Whitman's hand as if it were some strange kind of crab-like lizard that had now fastened itself onto her crotch. Finally, the lizard let go.

"Hey Rogers," Whitman said. "What did you think?"

"About your talk?"

"Yeah."

"Very interesting, but I wanted to ask you about something you said."

"Sure, man, but can it wait? I've got to go do something now. I'll be back in ten or fifteen."

With Whitman it was always ten or fifteen, or twenty. Just like that he was alone again. He looked at the other members, some of whom were dancing to the Beatles' "Across the Universe," which Rogers didn't think was made to dance to. He was startled to notice how many of them looked to be in their fifties or sixties.

"You having a good time?" Audrey said to him.

Rogers nodded. "I'm kind of surprised at the age of the members."

"You know more about death the closer you get to it," she said. "We think of old people as sacred."

He nodded. He supposed there might be some truth to what she said. Meanwhile, Whitman was giving a plastic bag to a pretty blonde on the dance floor who was handing him some money.

"You see that guy self-dancing?" Audrey said.

"Who do you mean?"

"The gray-haired guy with the triangular hat and purple jeans?"

"Yes."

"He's like the founder of our group. His name's Breman."

"I would have thought, based on how he spoke, that Whitman was the group leader."

"Like I said, he will be. We're having a vote soon but we're not really about making power grabs or any of that bourgeoisie stuff."

"What are you about?"

"It's more like a process of realization and then how we adapt to what we learn. Does that make sense to you?"

"I'm not sure," Rogers said. "What is it that you're all realizing?"

"That Time and Space are infinite, that the world is infinite but we're not. Really we're just a blink in all eternity."

"What about the afterlife? Doesn't V.I.N. believe in that?"

"An afterlife is just a wish to join the infinite, Whitman says. But we don't talk about it. We try to only talk about what we know about."

"Can't fault you for that."

She said something then that he didn't really hear. He was starting to get nervous because in the living room he saw Whitman dancing with the blonde, who looked much younger than most of the other women. A few seconds later, Whitman put his hands on her bottom and shortly after that began kissing her. Instinctively, Rogers looked at Audrey, who had an unsettled expression on her face.

"Hey, Roger," she said, misstating his name. "Want to come with me for a minute? There's something I want to show you."

Rogers shrugged and followed behind her, looking over his shoulder a couple of times at Whitman, who continued kissing the same woman.

"He's quite a dancer, isn't he?" Audrey said.

"I didn't notice."

"He always dances well with the new members, puts in that little extra six inches of effort," she said bitterly.

They reached the top of the stairs, where she walked authoritatively into a smallish bedroom. The next thing he knew, she was standing by the window pulling up the shade.

"Come here, Roger. Look out the window."

He went to the window, looked out with no idea what he was supposed to see, and saw only the black sky, the empty street, and a few stars.

"That's an exercise we have new members do. I learned it from the dancing boy."

"What is?"

"Looking at the night sky. What did you see?"

"Not much. It was pretty dark out."

"Did you see any stars?"

"A few."

"Each one of them is a world. What you saw was just a sliver of infinity, what Whitman calls 'the black map of nothingness.' We see a little bit of infinity and then we become a permanent part of nothingness, which right now doesn't sound like all that bad an option."

Rogers stole a look at her, afraid that she would start crying. She was at the window with one hand grasped tightly around the lock, the other rolled into a fist and resting on the ledge.

"Jesus Christ," she said. "Why do you guys always have to act like such fucking pigs?"

She means Whitman, Rogers said to himself, she doesn't mean you. People rarely mean you.

"I mean, I get it. In light of infinity, in light of nothingness, establishment morality is pretty ridiculous but we still can't help caring about the few people we get to know out of all the billions, we still can't help feeling what we feel, even if it is all ridiculous, can we?"

"No, we can't," Rogers said softly.

She turned and faced him, a sharp expression on her face.

"Do you know that I'm a shape-shifter?"

"What?"

"It's a kind of a magic thing, I guess, but the last time I was with Whitman, I ran into my room, locked the door, and a few moments later I turned into a rat scurrying along the floor."

"Scurrying along the floor?"

"Yeah, until I hid under the radiator."

"Come on. Why do you say something like that?" he said, his heart racing as he thought about the lizards.

"Because I did. I had my eyes closed the whole time so I can't be 100% sure. And it was only for a little while till I turned back into me again."

"Are you serious? I mean why would something like that happen?"

"I think it's 'cause I read a novel called *Rat* that was written from a rat's point of view."

"Was that by Kafka?"

"No, he did cockroaches. I was a rat, not a bug, and I know it happened."

Rogers only nodded this time, figuring she just wanted attention or sympathy.

"You don't get it, do you?"

"Probably not."

"You think I'm just making it up...Whitman gets it, at least. But what's the point of getting it if you act like a pig? What's the point of having the knowledge if you don't use it right?"

"What's the knowledge?"

"Of infinity. Haven't you been listening to a thing I've said?"

They heard the sound of people climbing the stairs then and looked at each other in the half light. Then she suddenly turned off the light. They listened to a mix of talking and laughter. It was Whitman and the woman he was dancing with, no doubt.

"Hey, who goes there?" Whitman said, still laughing. Rogers froze, saying nothing, as Whitman took a step into the room. "That you, Rogers?"

"Yes, it's me."

"How's the meeting going for you, bro? Seeing life a little differently now?"

Rogers said nothing.

"Hey, Audrey, didn't see you at first. OK, we'll use the other room," he said, pointing to the room across the hall.

"Whatever," Audrey said.

"OK, later," he said, his arm firmly around the woman.

"Hi, bye," the woman said.

"It's kind of like a metaphor for existence," said Whitman. "Rogers, this is Frances."

Hi, bye, he wanted to say, but didn't dare. Instead he merely said hello.

Whitman led Frances to the other room, partially shutting its door.

"Great, now we can hear them, too," Audrey said. "Do you mind if I close the door?"

"No, of course not," he added for emphasis.

"Oh, fuck it, let's leave it open."

"I don't get it, I just don't get it," Rogers said, pacing around the room, in the process partially drowning out the sex sounds coming from Whitman's room.

"What?" Audrey said, standing up. "What don't you get?"

"I don't get why it's bad to shut the door."

"Because it's small-minded. Because in light of infinity and how little time we have to live, we're not supposed to care about something like that, about who has sex with whom. We're not supposed to shut the door when we go to the bathroom either. You sure you want to join this group?"

Rogers stopped pacing. "I've always thought highly of Whitman," he blurted.

"Oh, yeah? What did he do for you? Give you a cut rate on heroin?"

"I just thought highly of him."

"Yeah," Audrey was saying. "Well, I thought highly of him, too."

"He's living his ideas," Rogers blurted.

"How convenient," she said.

Rogers said nothing. He decided then that he would try to leave but then he heard an odd sound from Audrey—something between hyperventilating and crying—and he froze a few steps from the door.

"What?" was all he could say.

"I said I'm going to turn myself into a hurricane and carry your Whitman away from you."

"You think I'm afraid of him, don't you?"

"More dependent than afraid, but afraid, too."

"I'm not afraid of him."

"Then go in there and be your own hurricane."

"He's busy."

"He stinks of lies."

"The man is busy, obviously."

"You stink of fear!"

"I'm leaving," he muttered as he left the room. But he stayed in the little space between the two bedrooms. He could hear Audrey pacing out of one ear and the sex sounds of Whitman and Frances with the other. It was like a bizarre stereo system that played a completely different stream of sound into each ear. He'd thought he would go downstairs and leave the house but he stayed frozen in place like a bishop on a chessboard. He could even see the bishop's monolithic face.

The sex sounds ended first. Audrey's pacing, on the other hand, was growing faster and louder. The next thing he knew he was knocking on Whitman's half-opened door.

"Yeah, bro, come in. No secrets here," Whitman said.

He wanted to see Whitman and he didn't, just like he was afraid to look at the woman but looked at her several times as if to verify each time that she was naked. He knew he was supposed to talk but so far wasn't able to.

"You want to score something, is that it?" Whitman said, sitting up halfway in bed, his genitals still visible.

Rogers wasn't sure what Whitman meant. Was he offering him Frances or some other woman? Was he a pimp, then?

"You want some E, maybe, or some good weed to pick you up?"

"You sell drugs?"

"Yeah, man. Good drugs at a fair price. Something wrong about that? At V.I.N. we prefer to call them 'consciousness helpers.'"

So that's what he was. Rogers had always suspected as much but hadn't allowed himself to think about it.

"I've gotta pee. Excuse me, guys," Frances said, getting up from the bed completely naked and walking into the space between the rooms where there apparently was a bathroom. He tried not to look at her but failed.

Whitman smiled in the half dark. "She's got a pretty ass, right?"

Whitman said as the bathroom door closed. Before Rogers could say anything there was a loud shriek from the other room, then the sound of running feet.

"Help," Audrey screamed, running out into the hall. "Help me! I'm on fire!"

Whitman sprang up from the corner of the bed, grabbed her hand, and ran with her into the bathroom. Rogers could see the flame—smell it too. The next thing he saw was Frances' hand over her mouth. She spoke a half muffled "Oh my god" as she ran naked out of the bathroom.

· · · · ·

Time passed but not as it usually did. It was as if it didn't register in his brain although many things happened. The fire that Audrey had set on her hair was put out. Audrey cried and Whitman comforted her and Frances joined them in a group hug (Whitman and Frances still naked) which Rogers watched from a few feet away. They offered to call an ambulance or drive Audrey home. But he guessed it was only a little fire and in the end Audrey left with Breman, the founder of V.I.N.

Then Rogers was walking with Whitman, down the same street he had followed him on earlier that night, the street that led to and away from the basketball court. There were no lights on the court and only a few lamps lit in the park. Whitman stopped near one of them at Roger's favorite bench.

"So, what can I do you for?" Whitman said, sitting down on the bench. Rogers remained standing. The phrase *midnight soldier at attention* popped into his head as if he were a sculpture with that title in a museum.

"You wanna buy something, right?"

"No, it was a misunderstanding. I don't want any drugs."

"OK, bro. What's up then? You look kinda frazzled."

"Never saw a person set herself on fire before."

"Oh, that. Yeah, that was a drag, but listen, you've gotta keep your perspective, man."

"What do you mean?" he said, not looking at Whitman's face but imagining his blue eyes (the same color as Rogers' father's) intensifying.

"I mean, infinity, the cosmic given. Weren't you paying attention at the meeting when me and Breman talked?"

"I wasn't sure I understood."

"Well, Breman's getting on in years and he's kind of losing it. You should vote for me in the next election. I'll make a much better leader. Anyways, this world has no end, man, and no beginning either, at least not one that we could ever understand. I mean, how could the world ever end? Where would it go? You got to get over your small thinking, man. You and Audrey, too. Our lives are illusions, man. Everything we dream of, everything we do, gets swallowed up by time and disappears."

Rogers felt stunned, stupid, but also didn't like being talked to that way, like Whitman was his father.

"It's not like I'm not aware of death. I'm not stupid, you know."

Whitman looked at him as if he were sizing him up. "I don't think you're stupid. I think, like the club says, you're a victim of infinity and nothingness. I want you to think about that some more. And also think about voting for me in next month's election. OK? Breman's too old and set in his ways. He just doesn't know how to reach a contemporary audience. So can I count on you?"

Rogers nodded, then wondered if Whitman had even seen it in the dark, so he said, "Yes, sure."

Whitman tapped him twice on his shoulder, said "Peace out," and left. Rogers watched his big, loping stride, wondered where he was going, then wondered how anything could really be contemporary in an infinite world.

It had gotten colder. The cold had snuck up on him like a thief. He hadn't dressed warmly enough, which meant he had to go home. He pictured his apartment and shivered. It would be a long walk, and there would be nothing there to look at—unless he saw the lizards again. Maybe he could stay in the park. He sat down on his bench and closed his eyes, trying to picture infinity, but after a little while he saw Whitman and Frances in the room when they were naked and then Frances disappeared and he saw Whitman's face, his big teeth smiling, his eyes blue and dark like the trembling sky.

Olympia

LATELY, WHENEVER I get up at night (for the usual reasons), I've gotten into the habit of writing down a line or two that spontaneously occurs to me as soon as I wake up. When I first write them down, these phrases often seem shockingly revelatory, but in the morning they invariably lose their impact and make only a small kind of private sense.

Opening my notebook, I see that last night's entry was no exception. More babbling about time and death and infinity. As if that weren't bad enough, I remember that Elle won't be coming today to do any cleaning or cooking, and feeling unusually lazy and hungry, even by my standards, I decide to walk to Hooperman's, a small Jewish delicatessen about a five minute walk from where I live. It's still warm enough, even though it's November in St. Louis, to sit at one of the tables outside, where I can eat my brunch and temporarily feel more connected to the world.

While I'm sipping my coffee and eating my corned beef on rye, the oddest thing happens. A very expensively dressed woman in black high heels and a purple blouse walks past me into the deli. She has exquisitely coiffed hair and expertly applied makeup (not something you see too often in St. Louis). She looks like she was plucked from a Park Avenue dinner party in New York and transported directly into Hooperman's. Of course I think of Olympia, who did live on Park Avenue, whereas I always lived on the Upper West Side among the struggling writers and perpetually arguing intellectuals, though I myself was a mere commercial photographer whose serious artistic work had thus far been almost universally rejected.

How did I meet Olympia? At a party in her honor in Sutton Place, where I had a kind of intermittent friendship with the host, Stephen Ivers. Stephen and I went to college together back when it didn't matter that his parents were ten times richer than mine because in college everyone believes they'll eventually become wildly rich and famous. Stephen invited me essentially so I could photograph his event for very little money, but I still eagerly accepted. There would be many wealthy people from the art world in attendance, he assured me. He made it seem foolish or perverse to pass up such an opportunity.

Olympia herself was one of the more widely photographed women in the world and was almost as rich as she was famous. She also owned a lot of art, though how many pieces were gifts, how many paid for, was a subject of debate. She'd already inherited millions from her businessman father when he died, which she more than doubled as a Broadway producer, and then in her middle age (though no one ever thought of age as something that happened to Olympia) she went to Hollywood and produced several hit movies that made her considerably more money. There was a rumor that she was a silent partner with Steven Spielberg in forming DreamWorks, but that was never completely confirmed.

Olympia was generally regarded as a kind of Renaissance tycoon. Many wondered why, with her dark-haired beauty and extreme charisma (which she displayed on a plethora of talk shows), she didn't act in movies herself. At times, it truly seemed she could do anything. But she also knew her limits. Perhaps her most indisputable gift, actually, and I say this without a hint of sarcasm, was as a creator of dinner parties, where her exquisite taste in décor was only matched by her chef's culinary creations. She was also regarded as an innovator for her unpredictable guest lists and daring seating arrangements that often resulted in new deals of consequence being made before the evening ended. There were always famous show business people at her parties, but there would also be distinguished lawyers, scientists, and writers—everyone from F. Lee Bailey to Woody Allen to Gloria Vanderbilt to Edward Albee. Olympia was a skilled conversationalist and a world class flatterer with the unfailing sense of just how risqué a joke to tell and, above all, how to act unfailingly interested in what her guests had to say.

Finally, Olympia was supremely gifted at cultivating members of the media (some of whom always attended her parties), so there was always a good chance that even her smallish dinners would be written about in the social pages of the largest newspapers, which people read then. (Television and the Internet have since ushered in a different kind of less gentle gossip.)

Although Olympia had her share of controversies in both her private and public life, she never drank or took drugs, which made people admire her more, and because she was disciplined enough not to complain in public, people invariably sided with her and wanted to go to her parties even more. For many it was the social highlight of their year, and I suppose for some, one of the defining experiences of their lives.

I was putting away my camera toward the end of the evening when Olympia, whom I'd barely spoken to before, approached me.

"Marty, I'm so glad you could come. I adore your photographs. I'm just speechless with admiration."

Having never received a compliment like that from anyone even close to her stature I was rendered pretty speechless myself.

"Marty, I wonder if, when it's convenient for you, you could take a few more shots of me in my home. The publisher of my new memoir has been hounding me for some 'personal images.' You know, to compliment the text."

"Of course, I'd be honored," I said, immediately regretting how florid I sounded.

"Marvelous," she said, flashing her most characteristic smile, the one always associated with a new success. "Then it's settled. And by the way, I'll make us a little lunch, if that's all right."

Then she gave me her card, and we agreed to meet three days later.

As soon as I was out of the building, I ran three blocks before getting a taxi, just to control my nervous energy. Then, ecstasy at my social coup was replaced by anxiety. I didn't know what to wear; I didn't know what to bring (besides my camera). I wouldn't know what to talk about, either. Later, I sought council from my friends, whose advice widely varied. Olympia had mentioned something about a bite to eat. Should I bring a bottle of wine?

Of course, too, I had read and heard the rumors about her amorous adventures with people who photographed or wrote about her (sexually, she was said to be quite wild), yet I didn't let myself think too much about what she might want from me beyond the shoot. It was just not the type of thing that happened to me—not that I was unattractive, just a bit unaggressive.

Finally, the grand day arrived as I entered her home—more like a palace than a townhouse. In the light of day, it was easier to see the intimidating photographs (all with tributes to her) of the dignitaries and celebrities that lined the hallways. There was Elizabeth Taylor, Tennessee Williams. There was Brando and Arthur Miller. I think Olympia both enjoyed and sympathized with my situation as she poured me an exquisite Grey Goose vodka cocktail with a twist of lemon. The drink helped, as did her fairly steady stream of compliments. She said she wanted most of the shots in her bedroom. After a few more minutes of conversation, we went there first.

Play it straight, I said to myself. If anything happens, she must make the first move.

But did I want anything to happen? Clearly I'd have loved to have her as a friend, but beyond that I couldn't imagine.

Though not overly large and more comfortable looking that one might have imagined, her room, where purple, orange, and red somehow coexisted harmoniously, was imaginatively decorated. There were none of her photographs on the walls, but I did notice two wooden dolls on her bed, one boy and one girl, each looking about ten years old and dressed as if going to school. I assumed they were hand carved in Switzerland or some Scandinavian country. They were beautiful dolls but they had a strange, almost overly sensitive expression in their eyes, as if they were young actors in an Ingmar Bergman film. I was going to ask her about the dolls, but she looked a bit concerned when I mentioned them, so I never discovered their origin. Later, I noticed that they were always on the bed table when we made love but never when she threw her parties.

"Well, I think we've taken enough shots," she said, looking me straight in the eye.

"Yes," was all I could manage.

"Would you like to spend any more time with me?" she said lightly. I noticed she was wearing her purple blouse. It was as if she suddenly came into focus as a beautiful woman, no matter how old she actually was.

"Sure. I'd love to."

"Would you like to go to the living room or stay here?"

I hesitated, as I often had when my mother would ask me a tricky question.

"Personally, I'd like to stay here," she said, "especially if we could lie down."

A moment later she shut off the lights, and we began kissing. A state of half-darkness was de rigueur for Olympia to make love. Meanwhile, at the bottom of the bed, the two dolls sat together as if conspiring.

When I got home and invariably thought about the previous night, I felt strangely happy, energized, even proud. But true to my worrying nature (which my father correctly told me I'd inherited from my mother), I began to see negatives and started to worry. There was not only the vast difference of fame and wealth between us, but she was considerably older than me as well. The very thing that made our relationship possible (the fact that I was much younger than her, which made her desire me) also made it inconceivable. Her age was something we never mentioned, as if it were something that only happened to other people. But other people did discuss Olympia's age, though mainly to marvel at how young she looked. She'd obviously had some world-class work done on her face, so people naturally wondered who her surgeon was and where and how exactly it had been accomplished, as if it had been a kind of sacred miracle. To a certain kind of rich person, the doctors who could do that were only a step from God themselves.

Like so many things in life, our first days were the best. We talked much more easily—she about various celebrated people, me mostly about my family. I remember enjoying that Olympia (unlike my mother, who was a world-class monologist) listened to me and even remembered the names of people I told her about as well as their roles in my life. Still, the central thing in our relationship was sex, where she was extraordinarily giving and adept in her own way, especially considering her age. She was definitely a kind of sexual innovator, at least in my modest experience.

I instinctively told very few people about Olympia, feeling she wanted our relationship to be private. One friend I did tell actually shook my hand and said "Congratulations," as if I'd just gotten a great review in the *New York Times*.

In those first few days, our relationship quietly amazed me. I was grateful; I was touched; but I always thought about her age, could never forget it though she looked beautiful and twenty to twenty-five years younger than she was. Still, the number repeated itself in my head like a mantra.

"Darling, I love you in bed," Olympia said one night on the phone, "but this has got to be more than that."

I knew what she meant, of course, but said nothing.

"We need to start seeing each other more than once a week, sweetheart, don't you think?"

"Of course," I said.

A short time later, we started going to expensive restaurants for dinners that she quietly paid for by slipping me cash just before we left for her place. Meanwhile, I continued to be her guest at all her dinner parties and accompanied her to various events ranging from art openings at the Met to Broadway shows to parties thrown by some of her endless stream of eminent friends. I was socially inexperienced, certainly by her standards, and once left her alone too long at a wedding reception in the Hamptons, for which I was bitterly scolded. Being alone for any length of time always seemed to terrify her. There was also the issue of my limited and therefore repetitious wardrobe. I remember that Olympia tried to partially remedy that situation by gifting me with an expensive sport coat, cashmere sweaters, and a black-and-gold watch romantically inscribed with the words "I'll take you there." Again, I was touched. I was enjoying her on many different levels, but her age continued repeating itself inside my head, accompanied by a strange sense of guilt. Neither of us ever talked about it. I sometimes felt like telling certain people at the parties who occasionally gave me skeptical looks that virtually all my past relationships were with age-appropriate women who weren't multimillionaires either and that I was drawn, like most men, to women who were younger. Moreover, I'd had an essentially good relationship with my mother, though she was admittedly somewhat possessive of me, and I wanted people to know that I was, when all was said and done, a healthy heterosexual hoping to find a serious partner with whom I could eventually have a child.

Meanwhile, as I was having these thoughts, time was passing, and I was also getting older, but without the cash to "halve" my own age as Olympia had. I hated myself for thinking about her age all the time (how disappointingly bourgeois of me, I thought), especially since I knew I had strong feelings for her of some kind, yet I couldn't help it. And so I continued my New

York social life with her as her, by now, absurdly undistinguished constant companion. My name began to appear occasionally in the *Post*'s notorious Page Six. Worst of all, chatting with Norman Mailer or Dianne von Furstenberg excited me in spite of the ultraliberal, almost Marxist way I was brought up by my idealistic father.

"Are you being faithful to me, darling?" Olympia suddenly asked while we were lying in bed (next to her dolls) watching TV in the half dark.

"Of course," I said, lying in a fairly convincing way, I thought.

"Well, I know how men are, and you're such a sexual person that I guess I'd understand."

"But I just told you I'm being faithful. Are you?" I said in an anxious voice that surprised me.

"Of course, sweetheart, I love being faithful to you. I think monogamy is a beautiful thing."

I didn't bring up, of course, the celebrated love triangles she'd been a part of, although those were years in the past.

"If I'd met you fifteen years ago you wouldn't give me the time of day," I said.

"Of course I would. That's a ridiculous thing to say and also quiet cruel, darling."

"Olympia, we both know it's true."

"I would definitely give you the time of day and a lot more besides. Want me to show you right now, darling?"

I really didn't "cheat" on Olympia much, and never with anyone that could lead to anything serious. When I told one woman that I knew Olympia, she seemed more interested in her for the rest of the night than in me, even after we had sex. I think there was a naïve or silly part of me that was fascinated that someone as renowned as Olympia could be cheated on by such an obscure being as me. But it wasn't just that. The age thing was always there, too.

In bed, she often allowed me to be the dominant one (which excited both of us) as we explored numerous fantasies. When it was time for orgasms, however, ours became a largely oral arrangement. (Intercourse sometimes hurt her and so we eventually abandoned it.) She was, however, superb and open to all kinds of experiments as long as they happened in the half dark. I quickly realized the darkness obscured her one admitted vulnerability, namely, what she considered the slackness of her flesh, which she used lighting and silk robes wrapped at strategic angles to camouflage. It made for a little awkwardness but nothing serious. Besides, I was having all kinds of intoxicating taboo sex with a world-famous woman (and fame ultimately trumps age, especially when the older woman looks and often acts so much younger). I sometimes thought that famous people are more alive than the rest of the species because they're the people the masses focus on so much. It's odd to watch so many people giving over their time (the only asset they really have) to vampiristically following the expensively created and very expensively maintained "beautiful people," as they used to be called.

When we were alone in her apartment (she actually owned two in the building, but the street-level one was strictly for business) we often ate Chinese food or sometimes simple dishes that she cooked. We talked a lot about our pasts then. She spoke of her famous husbands (she'd had four of them) and her regret that she never had a child. I talked about my family, my always-traveling father, my sister, who I now rarely saw, and my mother, who I saw too much, I suppose—at least Olympia thought so.

Once when I was drinking Grey Goose and talking about my

mother, I started to tear up a little and Olympia got alarmed. Strong expressions of emotion that didn't take place during sex disturbed her.

"Darling, please stop," she said, putting her hand on my knee. "You have me now."

I looked at her long fingers. I was struck by how thin they looked and how old. That was one part you couldn't get work on to look younger, and so it was like they belonged to a different person, these long, aged pianist's fingers that looked twenty-five years older than the rest of her. Yet they felt oddly comforting on my knee, as if they'd always belonged there. Later, she told me how she'd been abused in two of her marriages. It was a heartbreaking story.

"I love you," I heard myself say.

"I love you, too, darling."

I was going to say some variation of "If you met me fifteen years ago, you wouldn't have given me the time of day," but I didn't. (I knew it was true, anyway, and so just let it be.)

* * * * *

Since I liked to watch sports or political talk shows and she enjoyed old movies or reality TV shows (one of which she had co-created or co-produced), we often watched TV in separate rooms. Once, thinking she was lonely, as I was, I walked into her room. Her TV was on mute and her bed table light was off. I soon realized she was asleep. At last, Olympia alone and unprotected, unless one counted the dolls now positioned on her bed table that seemed to be guarding her. I gave in suddenly to a powerful urge to study her face up close and slowly approached her in her enormous bed. For several seconds I watched her sleeping face, now free of makeup. Her eyes were closed, but her face still looked lovely, though older, of course. I was fascinated, as if I were viewing a sacred exhibit in a museum.

Suddenly the bed table light went on. It was as if her dolls had warned her.

"What are you doing?" Olympia said, folding her hands over her eyes like a bird folding up its wings.

"I just came in to visit you."

"You were staring at me, weren't you? Did you take a picture, too? Others have, you know, and then sold them."

"God no. It was nothing like that."

"Don't ever do that to me again. Sneaking up on me while I was sleeping."

"No, of course, I promise I won't ever do that again."

"I can't bear it when people do that to me. That's why I've stopped sleeping next to men. I thought we had an understanding about that."

"I'm sorry."

She turned, still covering her face. "I thought I could trust you but obviously not."

"You can trust me."

"So, did you get your money's worth?"

"What do you mean?"

"Was it too terrible what you saw?"

"No, of course not. You looked beautiful."

"You won't get nightmares tonight?"

I laughed a little. "You looked beautiful. You really did. You always do."

Finally she turned to face me, holding out her arms to hug me. "Oh, I can't bear to be angry at you—you're far too lovely a boy."

At forty, it was the first time I'd been called a boy in years, and I kind of liked it.

"You must swear on your mother's grave to never do that again," she continued. "Knowing how important she is to you, I'll know you'll mean it."

"I swear…on her grave." (Although, my mother was still alive.)

"I'm sure from what you've told me she wouldn't like it either."

It was our worst fight, though not our last one. She sometimes correctly accused me of subtly flirting with a few of her younger female guests at parties, though she once sat in the back seat of a limo kissing and fondling a powerful director she'd produced a movie with while I just sat silently next to them trying to look at the street but for the most part failing.

When we finally got home (meaning her home, of course), I said, "You have quite the double standard, don't you?"

She laughed one of her stage laughs.

"Do you mean in the limo?"

"Yes, I do."

"*That* made you jealous?"

"I did feel a little neglected."

She forced out another fake laugh. "But darling, he's eighty-one years old. You can't be jealous of him. We kiss just as a kind of joke now, an act of kindness on my part."

"He's extremely powerful, famous, and wealthy."

"But sweetheart, so am I. You're being ridiculous. Now come into my room. I think I know just the cure for you."

● ● ● ● ●

"Darling, I've been thinking about your career and what we can do to get your serious work known by more people."

"There's no magazine or book that will publish my photographs, and no gallery that will show them, either," I said matter-of-factly.

"But sweetheart, you mustn't think so small. Your photographs are too good for any magazine or ordinary gallery. They belong in a special gallery. In Lee Witkin's or Castelli."

"Leo Castelli's gonna have a show of my neorealist work? Are you serious?"

"Yes, why wouldn't he?"

"Because he's the kingmaker of the avant-garde. Ever heard of pop art? He discovered it or was the first to showcase it."

I looked at Olympia, who appeared to be figuring something out.

"Well, maybe not Leo, though I always thought he rather liked me, but I've thought of someone else who's just as good as Leo, if not better. Someone who owes me a favor" (Olympia's term for someone she had had sex with).

"Who's this?" I asked, not believing her plan, based as it was on the theory that long-ago sex with a socialite would amount to anything in an increasingly cash-needy art world.

"Just leave it to me, darling. I'll take you there," she said with quiet conviction. Except during sex, she wasn't one to raise her voice. She didn't exactly take me *there*, but she did get me a kind of show. She found a respectable gallery owner uptown who agreed to an exhibit of "Selected Works from the Collection of Olympia." I was moved and bought her a scarf and an expensive necklace—at least, expensive by *my* standards. I had always been determined to spend as much money on her as she did on me. I wouldn't take advantage, I vowed to myself.

The show featured seven of my works and also, as I expected, a much larger number of photographs and paintings of her friends, from Annie Leibovitz to Robert Mapplethorpe. She said it was the gallery's idea to feature so many works about her to give the show "thematic unity." It was probably true but despite being dwarfed by such celebrated company, I was very grateful, though I received only a mildly enthusiastic mention or two in the review, which mostly centered on Olympia's "fabulous career." (No one seemed to notice the fact that she had merely bought the art, not created it.)

As she had done with such skill in the past, Olympia had the uncanny ability to appear to be doing you a favor while actually benefiting more from it herself. This was extremely evident at the party she threw for the gallery. Though I was supposed to be the guest of honor, everything soon centered around Olympia. Shortly thereafter, I began to realize that my desire for her was waning. Part of it was her ever more frequent mood swings. As it was near Thanksgiving she blamed the dreaded holidays. The mood swings often occurred right after her parties, as if she were crashing from a drug, and sometimes they culminated in quiet crying. Other times, she went into rages directed at various showbiz rivals. I began to see her less and less as a vibrant spirit and more as a prima donna or, in today's parlance, a self-pitying diva. She was asking me less and less frequently about myself, and when I answered a rare question about my life she seemed to be paying only perfunctory attention. Also, she wasn't only looking older, she was clearly getting older, too. We still had sex, but not as often or as well.

I had been with Olympia over three years now and was getting older myself. I began to think virtually every day about how I could extricate myself from her and return to my anonymous life as a commercial photographer living among my brethren on the Upper West Side. Someone who had a gallery downtown and who knew about me and Olympia offered me a show centered around "The Private World of Olympia." My prime role, I surmised, would be to solicit art from her innumerable friends, whom the gallery owner assumed I knew. Even if I did know many of them, it was an entirely superficial knowledge, since I was more of a curiosity to them than anything else. At any rate, I was now too proud and angry to accept the premise of the show.

Meanwhile, Olympia, who never liked Christmas, despite its accelerated social schedule, was complaining more than usual about "the horror of the holidays." One night she told me why. Olympia had always wanted a baby (I knew that before I met her), but only one of her husbands was willing. While watching the TV news, she'd just found out that that ex-husband had suddenly died. She was lying in bed in her purple silk bathrobe, head up on three satin pillows, holding her favorite dolls, while she continued to stare at the TV, though the news item was no longer on.

"I'm so sorry," I said, taking her hand.

She released hers after a few seconds. It felt cold like a mummy's.

"I can't believe Christian's gone. He was the love of my life."

I had heard her say this about at least three of her husbands. I didn't think she'd seen Christian in at least ten years. He was only a minor actor in the movies—the least successful of her husbands, which, it was rumored, was why they'd divorced.

"Christian was right," she cried out. "Why didn't I see it?"

"Right about what?"

She looked at me as she'd never looked before, and I realized she wasn't acting.

"We could have had a baby. He wanted one, too."

I nodded, feeling especially stupid.

"I had so many chances and yet I didn't do it. Instead, I had three abortions," she said, almost yelling as she held out three of her long, thin fingers as if each were a chance or a child.

"Now I'm old," she whispered. But because she whispered it, I wasn't sure she'd actually said the word "old."

She got up from the bed, and I followed her out to the living room.

I did my best to comfort her that night while I listened to her memories of Christian mixed in with fantasies of herself as a mother. She described herself walking in Central Park with her little boy and girl "Because," as she said, "I always wanted one of each."

"It's funny," she said to me later that night, "a mother is all I really wanted to be. And Christian saw that, he saw what was really inside me."

I looked at her standing by photographs she must have recently hung of Judy Garland on one side, Swifty Lazar on the other. It was hard to picture her sans her show business life.

"And for that crushing insight, I punished him horribly."

"The abortions?"

For a moment she looked at a newly placed photograph Richard Avedon had taken of her.

"Of course. I felt such guilt about it, which people felt in those days. In my sillier moments, I used to worry that people thought I was frigid."

"Frigid? You? Hardly."

"Yes, but people might have thought so with four husbands and no children."

"What would being frigid have to do with it?"

"That I wasn't having sex because I didn't like it, which is why I didn't have any children. Don't you see? I heard people gossip about it at parties."

"*You heard* them?"

"Well, my spies did. You must always have spies when you're well known in New York. Anyway, later, as the press got freer..."

"You mean more vulgar."

She smiled. "Yes, more vulgar. They began to write or at least imply that I was infertile, when nothing could be further from the truth, of course. You have to understand, it was a different time then."

"No, not so different," I said softly, though secretly I agreed with her.

"Abortion was an unspeakable sin—it was regarded as nothing less than murder. And yet I did it for my husbands. They said it would ruin my career if I didn't but what they really meant was *their* careers. Christian alone loved me for who I really was or could be, but I destroyed that, too."

"Why?"

"Because he was too young and handsome. And I was jealous, and people told me in one way or another that he was only after my money. Someone is always after something, aren't they? Of course I don't mean you, sweetheart," she added, in a strangely brittle voice. "But, fool that I was, I believed them because of my own ridiculous fears. Well, maybe not so ridiculous. People have always been after my money. Anyway, I felt I had to cheat on him to leave him. When he found out he cried like a baby and then tried to overdose."

"What happened?" I blurted.

"Oh, he was saved! But are we ever really saved? He lived

all these years later and now he's dead anyway. Though he did manage to finally marry and have three children, which is more than I can say."

I used to think Olympia was like a fortress. Now I started to see gaps in her construction, some of which time itself had created.

We talked on into the night, not even turning on a light. Later I noticed that the dolls were gone. I actually never saw them again.

Something became still more profoundly different between us then. It was as if she no longer felt the need to act pleasant around me or to act at all. Was she still mourning Christian, or was she perhaps deeply regretful that she'd exposed herself to me? Was I, after all, the right kind of person to confide in? And if I were did it mean that in some way she needed me, perhaps was even in love with me? The possibility of that was disturbing, as was the possibility that in some way, I might love her, too. I closed my eyes and pictured myself always escorting her to parties or museum openings, events at which I'd either be pitied or ignored. The next thing I knew, I was phoning my mother, who Olympia always said I worried about too much. I talked to her for a very long time. It was shortly after that I began pursuing more photography jobs, however lowly and humiliating they might be. As fate would have it, I found out that my old friend Stephen Iver's brother, Walter, was starting a photography business in St. Louis and needed an assistant. Incredibly, he eventually hired me.

I was very lonely that first year and didn't expect to hear from Olympia, who was furious that I left New York, but she started writing and then calling me and eventually surprised me by flying out to visit. It seemed especially odd in a way since she'd only come to my apartment in New York a handful of times. There were reasons for that, however, just as there were reasons why she would only visit me in Missouri once. Although I always hired a cleaning service prior to an announced visit by Olympia, she found too many amenities missing (Olympia called them "basics"). I didn't have enough chairs—and certainly no comfortable ones. My desk was buried under a chaos of papers. I didn't have much concept of a sofa, and my kitchen, in Olympia's words, was "like an undeveloped country."

Still, her visit was far from a disaster, and I was glad for it. We did have one fight, shorter but also more bitter than we used to have. We also had what I considered essentially successful sex, though we only did it once and found excuses that seemed relatively convincing for why we couldn't do it more often. I was surprised, at the end, when she asked me to visit her in New York, surprised, too, that I thought I saw her fingers tremble. It was obvious that I'd have to go and I insisted that I pay. Less than a week later she sent me tickets for the following week, along with a new watch. This meant I had to buy her at least a bracelet, which nearly broke my bank account.

Nothing terrible happened during my New York visit, either, unless one counted her typical traumas, which were endemic to her social circle. As usual, I stayed in the background at her parties, though she seemed to enjoy showing me off in a physical sort of way. She no longer introduced me as a photographer or even as her collaborator (though, it's true we'd collaborated on very little).

After I returned to Missouri, she continued her habit of sending me clips from the New York Times with a brief note attached that read, "I thought this would interest you." Often they were articles centered around the need for young adults to break away from their parents not only physically, but economically and, to a degree, emotionally, too. Apparently, Olympia thought I was still too close to my mother, though I was now two thousand miles away.

Time passed, and I began to feel more at home in my job. (I was destined to be a steady but unspectacular photography store owner, who only showed his serious art in state or local art shows.) Olympia and I still called each other once or twice a month. We always said we loved each other on the phone, yet I often felt we were like two actors playing the part of lovers whose affair was already over hundreds of nights ago. Our affection was now as absent as her dolls. They were still hidden or perhaps lost but, in any case, missing, and she never talked about them again. (Once I dreamed they were in a bed with us and we were all waking up together, but I never told Olympia about the dream.)

· · · · ·

The elegant woman finally leaves Hooperman's holding a shopping bag, her jacket unbuttoned. I find myself turning to see her purple blouse. I also want to see her face, but she is wearing dark sunglasses. Now I feel a sense of frustration, though at my age, frustrations never last too long, except perhaps my frustrations at time itself. A month ago my mother died, while Olympia, to judge by the social pages she occasionally sends me without comment, is still going strong. Sometimes, I get the feeling that Olympia will live forever, as she herself predicted (albeit half-jokingly) several times. I used to think my mother would as well. Come to think of it, I never really pictured myself dying either. Now that my mother has died, my feelings about all this have changed, and I know that Olympia and I will also both die, though in very different ways with very different people near us. She'll be surrounded by many famous people, of course. When I die, though, the only person at my bedside will be my sister, assuming she's still living just a college or two from my store (I never married or had a child).

Still, I marvel that Olympia and I are both alive (which sometimes puts a smile on my face) and that for a while, at least, we managed to share an adventure that for some reason life decided we should go through together, or as together as people like us could ever be.

The Intruder

First a sound, like a door shutting. Then he sat up in bed, telling himself it was just a dream sound or, if not, then just a random noise the house made. It was 3 a.m. and pitch black in his room with a cold floor that would require slippers. He'd have to reach for the glasses on his night table while hoping he wouldn't knock over his cup of water that stood soldier-like among his many medications. That was far too much to do to investigate a random sound, but then he heard it again. Not the kind of sound a house made on its own, either. He had no gun (it would have contradicted his strict brand of pacifism), so what should he do? He turned on his bed lamp and picked up his cell phone so that if he heard another suspicious sound he could call 911. Then he walked out into the hallway in his bare feet to hear the noise better. Almost immediately, his feet started to feel like icicles, and he quickly turned to go back to his room to put on his slippers. Then he heard yet another noise similar to the first. He walked more boldly than he thought he would toward the living room until he realized the noise was coming from his basement.

"Who's there?" he said, opening the cellar door. "If you don't leave now I'll call 911. I have a gun too that I won't hesitate to use if I have to." He heard a scuffling sound, like someone crawling, pulled the string on the weak yellow overhead light, and saw a pair of legs that looked like a woman's on his cellar floor. When he got closer, he saw that the legs were encased in a pair of torn jeans.

"What are you doing here?" he said, pointing the cell phone at her. Her eyes were bright like his daughter Zoe's, and for a second he thought it was her.

"Don't shoot, mister, don't shoot."

"What do you want? What are you doing here?" Her face looked frozen and pitiful, yet angry, too.

"I just came here to sleep. It's cold outside."

"How did you get in here?"

"You got a hole in one of your bottom windows," she said, pointing vaguely into the dark.

"A hole that you made, you mean, is that what happened? You broke my window?"

"No mister, I swear I didn't. It was there already, I just reached up and unlocked the window."

"So how long have you been here?"

"Couple hours."

"How many times have you done this?"

She paused as if figuring out a math problem.

"Three times, three or four."

"You've been here three days?"

"No, just at night when it gets too cold."

He looked at her more closely. All his life women had lied to him, even his daughter— although why limit it to them, men had lied to him too. He looked around himself but nothing seemed to be missing, so she probably hadn't robbed him. There was nothing in the cellar worth taking anyway. He'd set it up that way on purpose in his house, intentionally living well below his means.

"You ever come upstairs?" he said, noticing that his hand had suddenly started shaking.

She looked confused and didn't answer. "I mean, when you broke into my house. Did you ever come up my stairs and take anything there?"

"No sir. I didn't do that."

"Why not? I'm old, I might not have heard you."

"No sir, I never took nothing from your house. I'm not a thief, sir."

"I know, nobody is, but you did break into my house. You admitted that."

"Just when it got cold. I didn't want to freeze to death." Instinctively he looked at her feet and saw that she was wearing dirty socks and what looked like cardboard shoes.

Then he moved a step or two closer and saw her shiver—more like an animal than a person, he thought. For some reason she reminded him of the poodle he'd had as a child, but he couldn't remember the dog's name.

"Please don't shoot me, mister, I know I did wrong. I'm sorry."

"I'm not going to shoot you, for God's sake," he said, as he moved still closer to her.

"You look extremely cold. Are you ill? If you had knocked on my door I would have helped you." She cried a little then, which made it difficult to understand her.

"I know," is what he thought she probably said. Cuddles, that was the dog's name. His mother had named it.

"Do you think you have a fever?" he said in a calmer voice.

"I don't know," she said, shrugging her slender shoulders.

"You can call me Arthur." He wanted to put his hand on her forehead to see how warm it was but didn't think he should. Instead he stared at her again in the half dark. She looked to be somewhere in her twenties, and in spite of her condition, rather pretty.

"You gonna throw me out, Arthur?"

"No, no of course not, you'd probably freeze to death." He looked at her closely again. "Can I trust you if I let you upstairs?" She looked at him strangely.

"Yes sir. You can trust me."

"What's your name? You haven't told me that yet."

"My name's Desdemona. But people mostly call me Desi."

"Anything to save a second or two," he said, disappointed that she didn't respond to his little joke. "Here, Desi, take my hand. Don't try to get up by yourself." It might hurt his back, but he bent over to help her stand.

"Thank you," she said, looking away from him.

"Do you think you can walk upstairs like this?"

"Yes sir, I can do it myself, I'm not hurt."

"No, no, you'd better hold my hand," he said, not wanting to tell her that it was he who needed her help.

"Thank you," she mumbled. It reminded him of a little bird call somehow, the way she said it. It was amazing how delicate some people were when they got inside a house. He watched her take a quick glance at his living room and then turn away as if she'd looked too closely at the sun.

"Why don't you sit over there on the sofa?"

"Yes, Mr. Arthur."

"It's Arthur, just Arthur," he said.

She still seemed afraid to look at anything, as if in the simple act of looking she'd somehow break a law. Then he realized that she smelled bad. She probably knew it, which could only contribute to her anxiety. He tried to visualize what was in his medicine cabinet. There were a lot of medications, but nothing that could get someone high (he'd stopped taking codeine months ago).

"Would you like to use my bathroom, freshen up a bit, take a shower maybe?"

"I'd like to use the shower, if it's all right."

"Sure. You'll find clean towels in the linen closet. It's at the end of the hall by the bathroom."

She got up quickly from the sofa. She probably had to pee, too, like he did. He watched her walk with a little limp. He didn't think she'd steal anything yet the whole situation was such an anomaly—such a violent break from his routine that he had to battle the temptation to listen at the bathroom door.

He wondered if she was holding anything as he walked upstairs. Maybe not a gun, but perhaps a knife. It was impossible to tell, like trying to look into the moon or the black sky around it. Perception fails, he thought, especially remembered perception, which was all of it.

He moved a step or two closer, thought he heard a little stream of water coming from her. He felt like a child spying on her but it was fun in a way, he couldn't deny it. It was like he'd entered a land where he was in a trance.

Good God, what was he thinking? He backed away a few steps from the bathroom, then felt unsteady on his feet. It was certainly not his typical night, so he sat down on the sofa, in the same place where Desdemona had sat before she left for her shower. He closed his eyes and saw strange images from his childhood— splash wars with his sister in the lake, dressing for church with his brother. How he would have loved to talk with his brother or his sister now. She was always especially good at giving him advice about unusual situations he wouldn't dare tell his parents about.

"Demand that she leave the house at once!" his father would have said in the pseudo-impassioned voice that he used more and more frequently as his legal career evolved. "The world is my courtroom" was his attitude.

"I just don't understand," his mother would have said more softly, but just as powerfully. How he missed her, though if Desdemona were black his mother would have been doubly horrified, might even have fainted and would certainly have cried— crying being her favorite form of theater.

Why, suddenly, all this nostalgia for his childhood? He tried to focus on how much Desi was telling the truth. Fortunately there was a functioning toilet in the cellar so she wouldn't need to go upstairs and use his bathroom. He closed his eyes and tried to remember if anything was missing from the basement but it was like trying to recall the shapes in a dream.

She came out of the bathroom then, fully dressed, though her jeans looked like rags. Perhaps she might be some kind of crack whore. She looked at him as if waiting to see what he'd do next but he was damned if he knew. It was much easier to talk to her when she was in his cellar. The issue of course was what did he do next about her? He couldn't turn her out in the street now (though he had every right to), not after he let her take a shower. But he didn't trust her enough to let her go to sleep in his house. She might have a knife he hadn't noticed that she'd use to slit his throat while he was sleeping.

"What are you thinking?" he said, feeling he had to say something. It got her to look at him at least. His daughter was like that too, always looking away when he asked her a question. Didn't she know it was the classic behavior of a liar?

"Your life is so different from mine," Desi said.

"Yes," he said. She yawned, but he couldn't blame her. He was exhausted himself.

"You must be pretty tired," he said. She nodded, stifling yet another yawn with one of her hands. The question remained, where would she sleep? He could give her Zoe's old room upstairs, but then they'd be on different floors and it would be harder to hear her if she should walk away with his things. The only safe arrangement was if she slept on the sofa.

"You trying to figure out what to do with me?"

"Pardon me?"

"You know, where to put me," she said, smiling. She looked at him fearfully as if he meant to put her out on the street again.

"How 'bout the sofa right here?"

"Sure," she said, smiling.

"I'll get you some bedding."

"Thanks, Arthur."

It had been a long time since he'd been alone in his house with a woman her age who was that attractive, not counting his daughter, of course, who last visited him just over two years ago and then for such a short time that it seemed like a dream, as memories often did.

· · · · ·

He couldn't sleep. He hadn't expected that, although he often had insomnia. He'd thought the strain of the night, the sheer shock of it, would exhaust him; the trip to his cellar alone should have made him sleep. He seemed to remember going to the cellar with Zoe during her last visit to search for some of her childhood toys. Or was it for photographs of them at the beach?

Finally he got out of bed and started walking. He tried to remember the last time he'd walked out of his house for anything beyond picking up the newspaper. He thought of George, his caretaker, who shopped for him. The old have money and the young have legs, he'd once said to George with a smile.

He could already see the dim outlines of her body on his sofa in the half dark. She was probably asleep. He sat down in an armchair opposite her, perhaps ten feet away, and soon fell asleep again himself.

* * * * *

It snowed. He hadn't expected it but it did. Usually trying to find someone to shovel it made him panic but now it seemed like a mysterious gift.

"Well, you can't go out in this weather," he said to her later. "It's way too cold out."

Desi thanked him but he turned away and pretended he didn't see her. She fixed them some French toast for brunch. He told her she could eat whatever she wanted. Later she made them peanut butter and jelly sandwiches and turkey vegetable soup. She ate quickly, tried not to do it too quickly, but after all who knew when she'd last eaten a decent meal.

"Sorry I'm making a pig of myself."

"You're fine, no worries. It's probably been a while since you've eaten anything substantial, right?" She nodded as if not wanting to disrupt her chewing.

Later they split half a bottle of white wine. It was too sweet but he liked the way it made him feel.

"I'm really grateful for everything," she said.

"Believe me, I appreciate the company."

"Who's that a painting of?" she said, pointing to the wall above the piano.

"My daughter. I think she looks a little like you, though she isn't as honest...ethically or otherwise."

"I'm not half that pretty."

"I see a definite similarity," he said. "You both have blue eyes."

"The eyes and the hair maybe, but that's it. Who did it?"

"Someone who worked at the art gallery I used to own," he said. "A kind of friend."

"What does she do, your daughter?"

"She works for a lawyer. No jokes, please. Anyway, she doesn't make much. Her boss is kind of a thief, as lawyers often are. She came over to get a loan from me, stayed one night, and left the next day. Haven't seen her since, and that was nearly two years ago. Though we talk," he added. "Never paid back the loan," he wanted to add. They sat in silence for several seconds until Desi said, "I haven't been home for a while either. Guess that's not a shock."

"Why's that?"

"My dad ripped me off."

"Really?" he said, leaning forward in his chair.

"Yeah, my dad is a weird dude. He used to like to get high with me."

"Really?"

"Yeah, really."

"So how old were you when you did that?"

"Fourteen or fifteen. He used to go down in the basement and give me a beer if my mother was home or else smoke some weed."

He shook his head, feeling he had to show disapproval but secretly feeling jealous. How could a parent and child do that together? If he ever suggested it, Zoe would have laughed in his face.

"Yeah, thing is, at the time I thought I was lucky to have such a cool dad. But then he got into the harder things, meth and stuff, and that's when he also got into my wallet, and the next thing I knew he had all my money."

"So is that when you left home?"

"Not exactly. More like a few weeks later."

"Jesus, he must be worried to death about you."

"I sent him a card. I don't think my dad worries about me that much."

"I'm sure he's worried sick."

"How can you know that?"

" 'Cause I'm a father and I worry if I don't hear from my daughter in a week or two."

"Well, fathers aren't all the same."

"What about your mother?"

"What about her?"

"Don't you think she's worried?"

Desi shrugged. Why give a child such a fancy name as Desdemona if you were going to ignore her, he wondered.

"My mother's actually dead. Cancer," she said.

"Oh," he said.

· · · · ·

He dreamed he was chasing Zoe up a hill. She was made of part letters, part animals. Then she started running like a reindeer though the streets of a village whose buildings were old but also oddly sterile in a way.

"It's crazy," he said, by way of explanation to two or three people who noticed him chasing the strange looking child.

When he woke up, his heart was pounding but he was smiling. There was still snow and ice on the ground. Desdemona had stayed a second night in his home. He could hear her snoring lightly on his sofa.

He was happy and he was unhappy. He felt like he was dancing a jig: when he landed on his right foot, he felt happy, and when he landed on his left, he felt unhappy, fearful even. He was afraid that he would catch Desi stealing something from his house and then she'd have to leave. Yet he refused to spy on her, although he kept his eyes on her a good bit, as he had done to Zoe when he went through her desk and coat a few times. Once, he even looked through her pocketbook. He found some rolling papers in her wallet once and another time found some marijuana in her bureau drawer. Didn't know what to do then. Felt obligated to warn her or even punish her but felt ashamed of what he'd done, like a cop planting evidence—he, the great liberal patron of the arts—and so never said anything directly about it and hoped for the best. He told himself Desi wasn't a thief, just a homeless person who came into his house so she wouldn't freeze to death. She didn't go to a homeless shelter because they were so dangerous— she might be robbed or raped there, who knew? It happened all the time and she was so young and pretty (the two words forming inextricably in his mind together these days) and still naïve, no more street smart than his daughter had been, probably less.

* * * * *

"So what are your plans exactly?" he said, adding the word "exactly" because he didn't want the ambiguous answer that women often gave him. She looked puzzled.

"I mean, where are you planning to ultimately go?" She looked down at the floor. His punishment, he supposed, for shaming her with his question.

"What are you thinking? You've grown stone silent," he said.

"I'm wondering what it is you want from me."

"Only good things. What else?"

Desi shrugged. "I'm wondering if I could stay another night?"

He suddenly wished he could call a friend or two on the phone to discuss the situation. Someone he could ask for advice. But there really weren't such people around anymore. One way or another they'd left his world, or the world in general. Anyway, he'd gradually stopped calling them after his fight with Zoe.

"Arthur?"

"Yes?"

"You got anything at all I could eat? A piece of toast or something?"

"Will waffles do?"

"Sure," she said, smiling broadly. It was so easy for food to make her smile. In a way it made him jealous. I have spent a lifetime studying art, and waffles—frozen, mass produced ones—provoke a bigger reaction than I do, he thought. I am less than a waffle to her.

Strictly speaking, it was an uneventful and yet magical day. She mostly watched TV and read the supermarket tabloids she asked him to buy for her. Mostly they were silent but when they did talk it was easy. There was no more discussion of crime or punishment. Perhaps he should have adopted this policy with Zoe or his ex-wife but then, it wouldn't be wisdom if it didn't come too late.

He began to be uncertain how long Desi had been in his home.

He was sure of the last three days and often recalled "events" or vignettes from them: showing her where the bathroom was on the first night or, even earlier that night, saying "If you had knocked on my door I would have helped you." It was on the third night (probably not the second) that he hugged her good-night. He felt the wordless kind of beauty he used to experience looking at a Rembrandt or Monet.

It was odd how he often remembered things more clearly from his youth compared to events the week before, but it was the same with Desi. One day the photograph of Zoe fell down on his bed table when he pushed it accidentally while reaching for some grape juice. He was going to stand it up on his table again but instead put it face down in the table's drawer. That night, either the fourth or fifth, he talked to Desi about his daughter for a long time. He probably couldn't help boring her a bit but she acted interested and was always polite when she asked him what went wrong. He remembered shrugging his shoulders, not a typical gesture of his, before speaking.

"When I look back on it, it was like one day we were walking in a sunny open field of some kind and the next day we were walking through a mist or fog." Her blue eyes intensified as if she was picturing both images. Maybe he shouldn't have described it in such a literary way, but she seemed to understand.

"I know what you mean," she said. "It was kind of like that with my dad, minus the sunny field part. It was like as I got older he separated more from me except when he needed money."

"What about your mother?"

"My mom died a long time ago. When I was like fourteen or fifteen."

"Yes, I'm sorry, you told me."

"She had cancer, so…"

"Of course." The old like to forget about death, he wanted to tell her by way of explanation.

．．．．．

He decided to stop hanging around the bathroom while she took a shower. He knew he did it just to be close to her in a nonthreatening way. He remembered once when he accidentally walked in on Zoe. She was fairly well protected by her bubble bath, but she screamed anyway.

"Dad!"

"I'm sorry," he mumbled, turning his back as he rushed to the door. "Didn't know you were in there." Later he wondered if he should have added "I didn't see anything."

"Really dad, just forget it," she said in a tone of mild annoyance later. He nodded, said nothing more about it, and began concentrating on making her oatmeal. Odd how not many years ago when she was a little girl he'd seen Zoe naked almost every day and neither of them said a word about it. It was different when she was older of course. When you saw a woman naked it was now always a shock for everyone involved. And yet his generation had invented streaking. Nudity and innocent humor brought together, or so it seemed.

．．．．．

Can the old still be happy, he wondered? With so many pains scattered about them, hardly a square inch of flesh missing from their museum of pain, not to mention regrets (none of which you can do anything about, of course), the people you hurt who you wanted to love, the words (swords really) you couldn't take back. Lost women, lost wife, lost daughter. Your mind focused on medications all the time or simply on not falling once you mustered up the resolve to move at all. To move or not to move becomes the new *Hamlet* question. And who to believe or not to believe? Criminal how many doctors lied to you, "misdiagnosed" you, hustled you—made you want to kill them with one Hamlet-like thrust of your sword. It was the way of the world, of course. The world is seven billion times your pain, he thought. The world is a nightmare from which you will never wake up. Art or the study of art could never express this.

So all this and yet the tiptoeing, stutter-stepping, stumbling way he saw Desi in Zoe's childhood room made him happy like he was as a boy on the beach once. All of his life now somehow captured in that word "once."

· · · · ·

She wanted to go shopping. He wanted to be with her, of course, but didn't think his legs could stand it. Still, he told her yes.

"No, I didn't mean with you. I'm sure you've got better things to do," she said.

"I don't," he wanted to say. "I don't have better things to do. Take me with you."

"I just want to get some underwear and things, you know, lady things at a lady store."

"Of course," he said lightly, learning from Zoe it was better not to press at such moments.

"Let me help you out a little," he said, handing her a fifty.

She looked stunned, almost overwhelmed. "Thanks so much, Arthur. Thank you!"

He smiled. "You sure you'll be all right?"

"Great now," she said, waving his fifty in the air.

The young search for aloneness, he thought, and when they're old they find it.

Somehow the hours passed. They always knew how; like migrating birds, it was built into them. It was us who didn't understand the hours, he thought.

"Why am I thinking such garbage?" he said, sitting up in his living room recliner which was arranged so he could peer through the picture window and thus see Desi walking when she got back. It was the same chair where he used to wait for Zoe. There wasn't much to see on the streets. Not many sightings, though he valued every one, however banal. Without the sightings he'd go straight to memory and that wasn't a risk he wanted to take, not with Zoe and Desi both gone.

That night Desi was in a good mood (who knew the last time she'd bought something for herself?). They told ghost stories, of all things, drank lemonade, sang songs, and played Parcheesi. When they hugged good-night in the hallway he felt himself tremble, but didn't think she noticed.

The next day, they had one more day of peace. Then she wanted to go shopping again. He gave her a hundred-dollar bill.

"Wow!" she said, holding up the bill and staring at it, as if it were a work of art. "A hundred's a lot."

"You can't get anything decent for less than one hundred dollars. In fact, what the hell, I had a good week in the market. Today, take another hundred."

She squealed with delight. "Really?" Then she said, "Just like that?"

"Some days start well. Just don't stay out too late, maybe be back by eleven?" She gave him a funny look.

"Sure," she said softly.

. . . . .

Waiting for Desi felt just like waiting for Zoe, but because his lower back problems had increased since Zoe left, it hurt more to go from his room to his seat in front of the window facing the streets. He told himself to stay in a good mood no matter what time she got back. (Don't do what you did to Zoe, the yelling, the accusations. Heartbreaking to think of that.) But the later it got the harder that was to do.

Finally at 1:15 a.m., Desi opened the door with the spare key he had given her.

"Where the hell have you been?" he exploded, surprised by how quickly he was able to rise to his feet.

"Just out, like I said."

"But we had an agreement. You were supposed to be here by eleven."

"I don't remember saying that."

"You did! You said it and we agreed to it and I've nearly had a nervous breakdown worrying about you."

"What are you so worried about? Why are you so, so worried?" she said. Then noticing his chair, she added, "What, did you sit in that chair all night so you could spy on me?"

"So I could see you."

"Wow, I didn't know I signed a contract," she said, walking past him as she went to the kitchen.

. . . . .

The next night she was out again. He worried about being able to sleep because of the pain in his legs and back and the fear that Desi wouldn't come back. Already he knew their future, he knew it as if it were an extremely realistic painting he was viewing in his gallery. There was nothing difficult about the future

159

when all he really had to do to see it was to see the past. He'd seen his mother crippled years ago—not that he'd ever given her enough pity. It was the nature of kids to be selfish. Part of what went wrong with Zoe, he supposed, but perhaps he had simply needed her too much. Life is adverse to solving things, though it camouflages problems temporarily with pleasure, he thought as he turned on his side.

How long had it been since Zoe told him she loved him—how many years? Once they got older, parents always yearned to hear those words, but they so rarely did. It was as if the children withheld it, knowing perhaps it was the greatest source of power they had.

But that night Desi came back only a little late. She even brought him a can of beer, and though his doctor told him not to drink, he shared it with her and had a few laughs in the kitchen.

For the next twenty-four hours or so (though he was alone for most of it) things were settled, even oddly domestic. Desi was not a hard worker but she cleaned up after herself and put the dishes into the machine. Of course, when she started putting on makeup (that he had paid for) he started to worry. In retrospect, though, he thought he'd done pretty well, something he could never quite do with Zoe.

But when Desi went out the next night and it got past 12:30, he started to suffer, could feel it in his knees and somehow in his stinging, watering eyes. By 1:15 he was ready to call the police. They would stare at him and say, "Sir, is she your daughter or granddaughter?", or smirk when they asked him if Desi was his "girlfriend."

"No, not at all," he'd say.

"What is she, then? A friend you took in from the street? Did you pay her, sir?"

"She was homeless—she would have frozen," he would say.

It would be awful, the humiliation, but by 1:30 a.m. he was ready to call them anyway, until with one last look out the window he saw a car parked across the street. A moment later, he watched Desi get out of it. The car stayed still until she crossed the street, then drove away.

He'd meant to be calm, certainly under control, but within a minute he'd thrown a glass-framed picture of Zoe (taken the summer she went to art camp) on the floor by the artificial fireplace. Its pieces spread as if they were crawling.

"What?" Desi screamed, looking at the glass-splattered floor. "You did it again!"

"You think this is late, you're crazy."

"I am not crazy!" he yelled, staring hard at her. "You are crazy! You broke into my house and lived in my cellar like a rat. The only crazy thing about me is how nice I've been to you."

"I noticed you liked hanging around the bathroom whenever I was using it. Hoping for a peek?"

"What?" he said, his face turning red.

Then she punched her thigh as if to wake herself up. "I knew this would happen," she said accusingly.

"What? That I would give you shelter?"

"Shelter doesn't mean you own me. No one owns me." He looked at the holes in her jeans and couldn't tell if she'd been in some kind of fight, or worse, or if the holes were meant to be there. For a long time kids had been trying to look as intentionally ugly or poor as possible. It began in the sixties, he supposed.

"Look," she said, "can I just stay tonight and I promise I'll leave tomorrow?"

"Of course you can stay. As long as you want."

"Thanks," she said as she walked past him to her room.

"I want you to stay," he added, but only after she'd shut the bedroom door.

* * * * *

He was walking into his tomb. He tried to pretend he was dreaming but he knew. He even tried to resist physically but there was only one direction—down—and that's where he was going.

Then he realized it was only a thought—a thought midway between dream and reality but still only a thought. He was lying in his bed, not a casket, but he could understand his confusion. Desi was still in the house but in the morning she'd be gone. With Zoe, he'd been shocked when she left, but now he expected it. You learn to be left, he knew that. Still, it wasn't too late to reason with her, though it would be difficult. How do you reason with such an unreasonable person in such an unreasonable world where in the end it hurt to walk or even to move slightly in your bed/tomb as you sought after the elusive god of sleep, who only talked to you now when you craved silence? Also, there was his pride to consider.

* * * * *

The sun was out. The day broke blue. He hadn't heard Desi leave—perhaps she was still in the house. He tried to move as fast as he could but getting out of bed was still like moving in slow motion, as it had been for some time. Still, for a few moments, he felt like he was playing a riveting game of hide and seek.

Somehow he made it out of his room. He looked to his left and saw that the bedroom door was open, so he walked in. He could still smell Desi in the room. Then he noticed that she had made the bed. He felt touched for a moment and wanted to thank her.

"Desi," he called out. "Desi, your room smells so good." No answer, nor did she answer his next three calls. There was no note, nothing. Just silent space. He felt unsteady—how foolish of him to go into her room before he took his medications. Did he think he was a young boy? His unsteadiness increased and he slumped against the wall, then slowly sank to the carpet. At first he thought of trying to get up right away, but in his new, oddly comfortable position he could remember things better, perhaps because he didn't have the constant distraction of trying to walk safely.

It was only when he closed his eyes now that he could see himself hugging Zoe again, then Desi, then both of them, his phantom daughters.

Who says the old don't feel passion? They don't know anything, he thought. Or do they?

ACKNOWLEDGMENTS

My special thanks and deep gratitude to Glenn Blake and Laura Kessler, and heartfelt thanks also to Doreen Harrison and Jessica Rogen for their assistance on this book.

The following stories originally appeared, in slightly different form, in these journals:

The Hopkins Review	"Don't Think"
Notre Dame Review	"The House Visitor"
Per Contra	"The Chill," "The Intruder," "Olympia"
Pleiades	"Of Course He Wanted to Be Remembered"
River Styx	"The Offering"
StoryQuarterly	"Uncle Ray," "V.I.N."